Ice froze Frank's veins.

He jerked open the fire door and stumbled into the hallway.

"Colleen," he screamed, racing back to her.

Hurling himself into the trauma room, he expected the worst.

She sat crumpled on the floor, her face twisted with fear.

"Frank," she gasped with relief. Tears sprang from her eyes.

He was on his knees at her side, reaching for her. She collapsed into his arms. He pulled her trembling body close, feeling her warmth. Hot tears dampened his neck.

She was alive. Relief swept over him. A lump of gratitude filled his throat. He hadn't lost her. Not this time, but he hadn't reacted fast enough. She'd almost died because of his inability to protect her.

He rubbed his hand over her slender shoulders. "Shh. I've got you. You're safe."

For now. But someone wanted to kill her. Whether she had been working with Trey or against him, he was determined to end her life.

Debby Giusti is an award-winning Christian author who met and married her military husband at Fort Knox, Kentucky. Together they traveled the world, raised three wonderful children and have now settled in Atlanta, Georgia, where Debby spins tales of mystery and suspense that touch the heart and soul. Visit Debby online at debbygiusti.com; blog with her at seekerville.blogspot.com and craftieladiesofromance.blogspot.com; and email her at Debby@DebbyGiusti.com.

Books by Debby Giusti

Love Inspired Suspense

Military Investigations Series

The Officer's Secret
The Captain's Mission
The Colonel's Daughter
The General's Secretary
The Soldier's Sister
The Agent's Secret Past
Stranded

Magnolia Medical Series

Countdown to Death
Protecting Her Child

Visit the Author Profile page at Harlequin.com for more titles

STRANDED

DEBBY GIUSTI

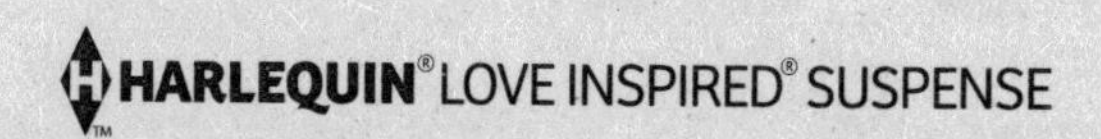

ISBN-13: 978-0-373-44655-1

Stranded

This edition published by arrangement with Love Inspired Books.

www.Harlequin.com

Printed in U.S.A.

Greater love hath no man than this,
that a man lay down his life for his friends.
—*John* 15:13

This book is dedicated to
Frank Forth,
a member of the
Greatest Generation
who fought in the
Battle of the Bulge.
Thank you, Frank, for your
service, your love and your support.

ONE

Gripping the steering wheel with one hand, Colleen Brennan shoved a wayward lock of red hair behind her ear with the other and glanced, yet again, at the rearview mirror to ensure she hadn't been followed. She had left Atlanta two hours ago and had been looking over her shoulder ever since.

Her stomach knotted as she turned her focus to the storm clouds overhead. The rapidly deteriorating weather was a threat she hadn't expected.

"Doppler radar…storms that caused damage in Montgomery earlier today…moving into Georgia."

Adjusting the volume on her car radio, she leaned closer to the dashboard, hoping to hear the weather report over the squawk of static.

"Hail…gusting winds. Conditions ideal for tornadoes. Everyone in the listening area is cautioned to be watchful."

The darkening sky and gusting winds added concern to her heavily burdened heart. She didn't like driving on remote Georgia roads with an encroaching storm, but she had an appointment to keep with Vivian Davis. The army wife had promised to provide evidence that would convince the authorities Trey Howard was involved in an illegal drug operation.

Hot tears burned Colleen's eyes. She was still raw from her sister's overdose and death on drugs Trey had trafficked. If only Colleen had been less focused on her flight-attendant career and more tuned in to her sister's needs, she might have responded to Briana's call for help.

Colleen had vowed to stop Trey lest he entice other young women to follow in her sister's footsteps. If the Atlanta police continued to turn a blind eye to his South American operation, Colleen would find someone at the federal level who would respond to what she knew to be true.

Needing evidence to substantiate her claims, she had photographed documents in Trey's office and had taken a memory card that had come from one of the digital cameras he used in his photography business, a business that provided a legitimate cover for his illegal operation.

She sighed with frustration. How could the Atlanta PD ignore evidence that proved Trey's involvement? Yet, they had done just that, and when she'd phoned to follow up on the information she'd submitted, they'd made it sound as if she was the drug smuggler instead of Trey.

Despite her protests, the cop with whom she'd dealt had mentioned a photograph mailed to the narcotics unit anonymously. The picture indicated Colleen's participation in the trafficking operation she was trying to pin on Trey.

Foolishly, she had allowed him to photograph her with a couple of his friends. A seemingly innocent pose, except those so-called friends must have been part of the drug racket. From what she'd learned about Trey over the past few months, he'd probably altered the photo of her to include evidence of possession and then mailed it to the police.

Too often he'd boasted of being well connected with

law enforcement. Evidently, he'd been telling the truth. In hindsight, she realized the cop had probably been on the take.

She wouldn't make the same mistake twice. No matter how much she wanted Trey behind bars, she couldn't trust anyone involved in law enforcement at the local level. For all she knew, they were all receiving kickbacks.

Later tonight, after returning to the motel in Atlanta where Colleen had been holed up and hiding out, she would overnight copies of everything she had secreted from Trey's office, along with whatever evidence Vivian could provide, to the Drug Enforcement Administration's Atlanta office. Surely Trey didn't have influence with the federal DEA agents, although after the pointed questions she'd fielded following her sister's death, Colleen didn't have a warm spot in her heart for cops at any level.

Glancing at her GPS, she anticipated the upcoming turn into a roadside picnic park. Vivian had insisted they meet in the country, far from where the army wife lived at Fort Rickman and the neighboring town of Freemont, Georgia.

Colleen glanced again at her rearview mirror, relieved that hers was the only vehicle on the road. Vivian was right. Meeting away from Freemont and Fort Rickman had been a good decision. Except for the storm that threatened to add an unexpected complication to an already dangerous situation.

Turning into the picnic park, Colleen spotted a car. A woman sat at the wheel. Braking to a stop next to the sedan, Colleen grabbed her purse off the seat and threw it in the rear. Then stretching across the console, she opened the passenger door, all the while keeping the motor running.

Clutching a leather shoulder bag in one hand and a

cell phone in the other, Vivian stepped from her car and slipped into the front seat. She was as tall as Colleen's five feet seven inches, but with a pixie haircut that framed her alabaster skin and full mouth, which made her appear even more slender in person than in the photographs Colleen had seen on Facebook.

Fear flashed from eyes that flicked around the car and the surrounding roadside park.

"Were you followed?" Vivian nervously fingered her purse and then dropped it at her feet.

"I doubled back a few times and didn't see anyone." Colleen pointed to the thick woods surrounding the off-road setting. "No one will find us here, Vivian. You're safe."

Rain started to ping against the roof of the car. Colleen turned on the wipers.

"I don't feel safe." Vivian bit her chipped nails and slumped lower in the seat. "And I'm not even sure I should trust you."

"I told you we'll work together."

"What if my husband finds out?"

Colleen understood the woman's concern. "He was deployed. You were depressed, not yourself. If you're honest with him, he'll understand."

"He won't understand why his wife accepted an all-expense-paid trip to a Colombian resort while he was deployed to a war zone. He also won't understand how I got involved with Trey Howard."

Colleen's sister had been as naive as Vivian. Briana had been used and abused by the drug dealer, which made Colleen realize how easily Vivian could have been taken in by Trey.

"My sister made the same mistake. Two other women

did, as well. That's why I contacted you. You still have a chance to escape."

Vivian glanced out the window. "My husband has orders for Fort Hood. We're moving in three weeks." She raked her hand through her short hair. "I'll be okay, unless the cops find out I smuggled drugs into the country."

"I'll mail whatever evidence you brought today to the DEA without mentioning your name or mine. They won't be able to trace anything back to either of us." Colleen rubbed her hand reassuringly over the young woman's shoulder. "Besides, you didn't know what was in the package Trey had you bring into the US for him."

"I knew enough not to ask questions, which means I could end up in jail." Vivian shrugged away from Colleen and reached for the door handle. "I made a mistake meeting you."

"Vivian, please." Colleen grabbed the young woman's arm before she stepped from the car.

A shot rang out.

Vivian clutched her side and fell onto the seat.

Colleen's heart stopped. She glanced into the woods, seeing movement. A man stood partially hidden in the underbrush, a raised rifle in his hands.

Trey.

A car was parked nearby. She couldn't make out the make or model.

"Stay down," Colleen warned. Leaning across the console and around Vivian, she pulled the passenger door closed.

Another shot. A rear window shattered.

Vivian screamed.

Fear clawed at Colleen's throat. She threw the car into gear and floored the accelerator. The wheels squealed in protest as they left the roadside park.

A weight settled on Colleen's chest. Struggling to catch her breath, she gripped the steering wheel white-knuckled and focused on the two-lane country road that stretched before them.

"He tried to kill me," Vivian gasped. Tears filled her eyes.

Colleen glanced at the hole in the window and the spray of glass that covered the rear seat. "He tried to kill both of us."

She should have known Trey would follow her. He loved fast cars, and no matter what he was driving today, her Honda Civic couldn't outrun his vehicle of choice.

Hot tears burned her eyes. "Our only chance is to find a place to hide and hope Trey thinks we continued north toward the interstate."

He'd eventually realize his mistake and double back to search for them. By then, they would have left the area by another route.

"I'm scared," Vivian groaned.

Refusing to give voice to her own fear, Colleen focused on their most immediate problem. "What's near here that could offer shelter? We need to stow the car out of sight."

"An Amish community." Vivian pointed to the upcoming intersection. "Turn left. Then take the next right. There's a small shop. An old barn sits in the rear. It's usually empty when I drive by."

Colleen followed the younger woman's directions, all the while checking the rearview mirror.

Vivian glanced over her shoulder. "If he catches us, he'll kill us."

"Not if we hole up in the barn. He won't look for us there."

The army wife pointed to the upcoming intersection.

"Turn right. Then crest the hill. The Amish store is on the other side of the rise."

Colleen's stomach tightened with determination. She turned at the intersection and kept the accelerator floored until the car bounded over the hill.

The rain intensified. Squinting through the downpour, she spied the Amish store. One-story, wooden frame, large wraparound porch. Just as Vivian had said, a barn stood at the side of the shop.

Colleen took the turn too sharply. The tires squealed in protest. A gravel path led to the barn. The car bounced over the rough terrain.

She glanced at the road they had just traveled. Trey's car hadn't crested the hill. Relieved, Colleen drove into the barn. Before the engine died, she leaped from the car and pulled the doors closed, casting them in semi-darkness.

Outside, wind howled. Rain pounded against the wooden structure.

"Help me." Vivian's voice.

Colleen raced around the car and opened the passenger door. The woman's face was pale as death. Blood soaked her clothing. For the first time, Colleen saw the gaping hole in Vivian's side.

Removing her own coat, Colleen rolled it into a ball and pressed it onto the wound to stem the flow of blood. Holding it tight with her left hand, she reached for her cell and tapped in 9-1-1.

Before the call could go through, a ferocious roar, both powerful and insistent, gathered momentum, like a freight train on a collision course with the barn. Even without seeing the funnel cloud, Colleen knew a tornado was headed straight for them.

The barn shook. Hay fell from the overhead loft. The noise grew louder. Colleen's ears popped.

Swirling wind enveloped them. Clods of Georgia clay and shards of splintered wood sprayed through the air like shrapnel.

She threw herself over Vivian, protecting her. *God help us*, Colleen prayed as the tornado hit, and the barn crashed down around them.

"Frank," Evelyn screamed from the kitchen. "There's a tornado."

Startled by the tremor in his sister's voice, Frank Gallagher pulled back the living room curtain. His heart slammed against his chest at what he saw. A huge, swirling funnel cloud was headed straight for her house.

"Get to the basement, Evie."

Her sluggish footsteps sounded from the kitchen as she threw open the cellar door and cautiously descended into the darkness below. Injured in a car accident some years earlier, Evelyn's gait was slow and labored, like a person older than her 42 years.

"Duke?" Frank called. The German shepherd, a retired military working dog, appeared at his side.

"Heel." Together, they followed Evelyn down the steep steps.

An antique oak desk sat in the corner and offered additional protection. Frank hurried her forward.

"Get under the desk, Evie."

A deafening roar enveloped them. Frank glanced through the small basement window. His gut tightened.

Debris sailed through the air ahead of the mass of swirling wind bearing down on them.

His heart stalled, and for one long moment, he was

back in Afghanistan. The explosion. The flying debris. The building shattering around him.

Trapped under the rubble, he had gasped for air. The smell of death returned to fill his nostrils. Only he had lived.

Duke whined.

"Frank," Evelyn screamed over the incessant roar. She grabbed his arm and jerked him down next to her.

Frank motioned for Duke to lie beside them. The thunderous wail drowned out his sister's frantic prayers. All he heard was the howling wind, like a madman gone berserk, as chilling as incoming mortar rounds.

He tensed, anticipating the hit, and choked on the acrid bile that clogged his throat. Tightening his grip on his sister's outstretched hand, Frank opened his heart, ever so slightly, to the Lord.

Save Evie. The prayer came from deep inside, from a place he'd sealed off since the IED explosion had changed his life forever. Just that quickly the raging wind died, and the roar subsided.

Frank expelled the breath he'd been holding.

Evelyn moaned with relief. "Thank you, God."

Crawling from under the desk, he helped his sister to her feet and then glanced through the window. Mounds of tree limbs, twisted like matchsticks, littered the yard. At least the house had been spared.

He pulled his mobile phone from his pocket. No bars. No coverage.

Evelyn reached for the older landline phone on the desk. "I've got a dial tone."

"Call 911. Let them know the area along Amish Road was hit and to send everything available. Then phone the Criminal Investigation Division on post. Talk to Colby Voss. Tell him the Amish need help."

"Colby would tell you to stay put, Frank. You're still on convalescent leave."

Ignoring her concern for his well-being, Frank patted his leg for Duke to follow him upstairs.

Another close call. Was God trying to get his attention? A verse from scripture floated through his mind, *Come back to me.*

In the kitchen, Frank yanked his CID jacket from the closet and grabbed leather work gloves he kept nearby. Pushing through the back door, he stopped short and pulled in a sharp breath at what he saw—a different kind of war zone from what he'd experienced in Afghanistan, but equally as devastating.

The tornado had left a trail of destruction that had narrowly missed his sister's house. He searched for the Amish farmhouses that stretched along the horizon. Few had been spared. Most were broken piles of rubble, as if a giant had crushed them underfoot.

A sickening dread spread over him. The noise earlier had been deafening. Now an eerie quiet filled the late Georgia afternoon. No time to lament. People could be trapped in the wreckage.

"Come on, boy." Frank quickly picked his way among the broken branches and headed for the path that led through the woods. He ignored the ache in his hip, a reminder of the IED explosion and the building that had collapsed on top of him. Thankfully, a team of orthopedic surgeons had gotten him back on his feet. A fractured pelvis, broken ribs and a cracked femur had been insignificant compared with those who hadn't made it out alive.

Still weak from the infection that had been a life-threatening complication following surgery, Frank pushed forward, knowing others needed help. Skirting areas where the tornado had twisted giant trees like pickup sticks, he checked his cell en route and shook his head with regret at the lack of coverage.

At the foot of the hill, he donned his leather work gloves and raced toward the Amish Craft Shoppe. A brother and sister in their teens usually manned the store.

"Call out if you can hear me," he shouted as he threw aside boards scattered across the walkway leading to the front porch. "Where are you?" he demanded. "Answer me."

Duke sniffed at his side.

"Can you hear me?" he called again and again. The lack of response made him fear the worst and drove him to dig through the fallen timbers even more frantically.

An Amish man and woman tumbled from a farmhouse across the street. Their home had lost its roof and a supporting side wall.

The bearded man wore a blue shirt and dark trousers, held up with suspenders. Dirt smudged his face and his cheek was scraped.

"The store was closed today," he shouted, waving his hands to get Frank's attention. "The youth are at a neighboring farm."

"You're sure?" Frank was unwilling to give up the search if anyone was still inside.

The man glanced at the woman wearing a typical Amish dress and apron.

"*Jah*, that is right," she said, nodding in agreement.

"What about your family?" Frank called. "Was anyone hurt?"

"Thanks to God, we are unharmed, but our neighbors are in need." The man pointed to the next farmhouse and the gaping hole where the wall and roof had been. He and his wife ran to offer aid.

Before Frank could follow, he glanced at the nearby barn. The corner of one wall remained standing, precariously poised over a pile of rubble. At that moment, the cloud cover broke, and the sun's reflection bounced off a piece of metal buried in the wreckage.

Something chrome, like the bumper of a car. The Amish didn't drive automobiles, but a traveler passing by could have been seeking shelter from the storm.

He raced to the barn and dug through the debris. "Shout if you can hear me."

A woman moaned.

"Where are you?" Frank strained to hear more.

All too well, he knew the terror of being buried. His heart lodged in his throat as the memories of Afghanistan played through his mind.

Duke pawed at a pile of timber, his nose sniffing the broken beams and fractured wood.

He barked.

"Help."

Working like a madman, Frank tossed aside boards piled one upon the other until he uncovered a portion of the car. The passenger door hung open. Shoving fallen beams aside, he leaned into the vehicle's interior.

A woman stared up at him.

"Are you hurt?"

She didn't respond.

Hematoma on her left temple. Cuts and abrasions. She was probably in shock.

"Can you move your hands and feet?"

She nodded.

"Stay put, ma'am, until the EMTs arrive. You could have internal injuries."

She reached for his hand and struggled to untangle herself from the wreckage.

"You shouldn't move, ma'am."

"I need help." She was determined to crawl from the car.

"Take it slow." Frank had no choice but to assist her to her feet. She was tall and slender with untamed hair the color of autumn leaves. She teetered for a moment and then stepped into his arms.

He clutched her close and warmed to her embrace. "You're okay," he whispered. "I've got you. You're safe."

"But—"

She glanced over her shoulder. He followed her gaze, his eyes focusing on a second woman.

Black hair. Ashen face. A bloodstained jacket lay wadded in a ball at her waist.

Pulling back the covering, Frank groaned. Her injury hadn't been caused by the storm.

She'd taken a bullet to the gut.

TWO

Where were the emergency response teams?

Police, fire, EMTs?

Frank removed his belt and wove it under the victim's slender waist. Determined to keep her alive, he cinched the makeshift tourniquet around the rolled-up jacket to maintain pressure and hopefully stop the flow of precious blood she was losing much too fast.

He glanced at the redhead hovering nearby. She looked as concerned as he felt. They both knew that without immediate medical help, the injured woman wouldn't survive.

"If you've got a cell, call 911."

She pulled a phone from her pocket and shook her head. "There…there's no coverage."

The gunshot victim needed an ambulance and needed it fast. Frustration bubbled up within him. After ten years with the US Army's Criminal Investigation Division, Frank didn't like the only conclusion he could make with the information at hand.

"Why'd you shoot her, ma'am?"

Red shook her head, her eyes wide. "I did no such thing."

He pointed to the demolished car. "This is your Honda?"

She nodded.

"How'd she end up in your car?"

"I…I stopped at the picnic park about a mile from here. She needed help. I opened the passenger door, and a shot rang out."

"Did you see the shooter?"

Red rubbed the swollen lump on her forehead. "I…I don't remember."

"Don't remember or don't want to remember?" Even he heard the annoyance in his voice.

The woman stared at him, her face blank. Maybe she was telling the truth.

"What's your name, ma'am?"

"Colleen…Colleen Brennan."

"You're from around here?"

"Atlanta."

Which didn't make sense. "But you just happened to pull into a nearby picnic park?"

Her green eyes flashed with fear.

Trauma played havoc with emotions and memory. Frank wanted to believe her, but he knew too well that the pretty woman with the tangled hair could be making up a story to throw him off track.

Duke sniffed at her leg. She reached down and patted his head.

A raspy pull of air forced Frank's attention back to the gunshot victim. She moaned.

Sirens sounded in the distance.

He leaned into the car. "Stay with us, ma'am. Help's on the way." Hopefully it would arrive in time.

Her glassy eyes focused on Colleen. Frank turned to stare at her.

The redhead blanched. The lump on her temple cried for ice, and the scrapes to her cheek and hands needed debridement.

"After your friend's treated, we'll have the EMTs take a look at you."

"I'm fine." Colleen's voice was lifeless.

Slipping past her, he waved his arms in the air at the approaching first responders. Two ambulances and a fire truck from one of the rural fire stations.

The emergency crew pulled in front of the Craft Shoppe. Frank motioned them closer to the barn, where they parked and jumped from their vehicles.

"Two women are injured." Frank pointed to the collapsed structure. "One with a bullet wound to her gut. She's lost blood. The other woman has a knot the size of a lemon on her forehead and could be in shock."

Hauling medical bags and a backboard, a pair of EMTs waded through the collapsed wreckage around the car. A second set of paramedics set up an emergency triage area near the second ambulance.

"We'll need you to step away from the car, ma'am," one of the EMTs told Colleen.

Her brow furrowed. She peered around them at Frank.

Seeing the confusion in her gaze, his anger softened. "It's okay," he assured her. "They're here to help."

Despite the niggling worry that Colleen Brennan may have been involved in the shooting, he reached for her. "Come toward me, and we'll get out of their way."

She offered him her hand. Her skin was soft, but clammy, which wasn't good.

"Let's see if someone can check your forehead."

She shook her head. "Vivian's the one who needs help."

"You know her name?" Although surprised by the revelation, Frank kept his voice low and calm. "What's her last name?"

"I...I don't remember." Colleen pulled her hand from his grasp. "We were trying to get away—"

She hesitated.

"Away from—" he prompted.

"A man. He was in the woods. Tall. Dark jacket. Hood over his head. He had a rifle."

"Did you see a car?"

She shook her head. "Not that I remember."

Selective memory or a partial amnesia brought on by trauma?

"Come with me." Frank ushered Colleen to the triage site. Duke followed close behind.

A pair of EMTs helped her onto a gurney pushed against the side of the ambulance. One man cleaned her hands and face and treated the scratches on her arms while the other took her vitals, checked her pupils and then applied an ice pack to the lump on her forehead.

"You've got a slight concussion, but you don't need hospitalization," he said. "Is there anyone who can check on you through the night?"

She shook her head. "I...I live alone."

"In Atlanta," Frank volunteered.

An Amish man stumbled toward the ambulance. Blood darkened his beard. The EMTs hurried to help him.

"You'll spend the night here in the Freemont area," Frank told Colleen. Before she could object, he pointed to the one-story brick ranch visible in the distance. "My sister, Evelyn, owns the house on top of the knoll. There's an extra room. You can stay with her."

"I...I need to get back to Atlanta."

"From the looks of your car, travel anytime soon seems unlikely. Downed trees are blocking some of the roadways and won't be cleared until morning."

"Is there a bus station?"

"In town, but you need to talk to law enforcement first."

The downward slope of her mouth and the dark shadows under her eyes gave him concern. She looked fragile and ready to break.

"I...I don't know your name," she stammered.

"It's Frank Gallagher, and the dog's Duke."

Her face softened for a moment as Duke licked her hand, then she glanced back at Frank.

"You're a farmer?"

He shook his head. "I'm an army guy. CID."

Seeing her confusion, he explained, "Criminal Investigation Division. We handle felony crimes for the military."

Her eyes narrowed. "You're a cop?"

He shrugged. "More like a detective. What about you?"

"Flight attendant."

"Hartsfield?"

She nodded, indicating the Atlanta airport.

One of the EMTs returned and pulled a bottle of water from a cooler. "I want you to sit up, ma'am, and drink some water. I'll check on you again in a few minutes."

Frank pointed to the nearby fire truck. "You relax while Duke and I talk to the guys from the fire department."

Rounding the ambulance, Frank glanced at the road. A line of first responders and Good Samaritan townspeople had arrived to help in the rescue effort. The scene farther south was probably the same, with people flocking to the area in hopes of aiding those in need.

Glancing back at Colleen, he was relieved to see she had closed her eyes and was resting her head against the side of the ambulance.

Static played over the fire truck's emergency radio. A tall, slender guy in his midtwenties stood nearby. He wore a navy blue shirt with the Freemont Fire Department logo and a name tag that read Daugherty.

His face brightened when he saw Duke.

"Nice dog."

"Daugherty, can you can patch me through to the local police?"

"No problem, sir."

Once Frank got through to the dispatcher, he explained about the gunshot victim. "Colleen Brennan was the driver of the vehicle. She'll be staying overnight at Evelyn Gallagher's house." He provided the address.

"Everyone's tied up with the rescue operation," the dispatcher explained. "I'll pass on the information, but be patient."

After disconnecting, he requested a second call to Fort Rickman.

"Did you want to contact the military police?" Daugherty asked.

"That works."

He connected Frank to the provost marshal's office. After providing his name, Frank requested all available military help be sent to the Amish area.

"Roger that, sir. I believe we've already received a request for aid, but I'll notify the Emergency Operations Center, just in case. They'll pass the information on to General Cameron."

"Any damage on post?"

"A twister touched down. Some of the barracks in the training area were in the storm's path. No loss of life reported thus far. The chaplain said God was watching out for us."

Frank wasn't sure he'd give God the credit. If the Lord

protected some, why were others in the storm's path? "What about Freemont?"

"We've got some spotty reports. A trailer park on the outskirts of town was hit with some injuries. A few shops downtown and a number of the old three-story brick buildings on the waterfront."

"The abandoned warehouses?"

"That's correct. We're awaiting more details from the local authorities. The information I received is that Allen Quincy is heading the civilian relief effort."

"The mayor?"

"Yes, sir. He's asked for our help. We've called in all personnel. I'll pass on the information about the Amish area."

"Let the Red Cross and medical personnel know, as well."

"I'm on it, sir."

"Do you have landline access?" Frank asked.

"To main post only."

"See if you can contact CID Headquarters. Ask for Special Agent Colby Voss. Tell him Special Agent Frank Gallagher is at the Craft Shoppe, located at the northern end of Amish Road. We're going to need him."

"Roger that, sir."

Colby's wife, Becca, had been raised Amish. She knew the area and the local Amish bishop, but Becca was on temporary duty out of the state so Colby was the next best choice.

He and Frank had joined the CID years earlier and had served together before. Frank could attest to Colby's ability both as an investigator and diplomat.

The Amish were a tight community and preferred to take care of their own. After the tornado, they needed help. Colby might be able to bridge the gap between the Amish and their *English* neighbors.

Frank thanked Daugherty for the use of his radio. He and Duke returned to the ambulance in time to hear the EMT reassure Colleen.

"Looks like dehydration was the problem, ma'am," he told her. "Your vitals are better so you're good to go."

"What about that lump on her forehead?" Frank asked.

"She should be okay, especially if someone checks on her through the night."

"It's nothing to worry about," Colleen insisted as she hopped down from the gurney.

Frank reached out a hand to steady her. She held on to him for a long moment and then nodded her thanks. "I'm okay."

"Ma'am, you need to take it easy for the next day or two," the EMT cautioned.

"And the gunshot victim?" Frank asked, his gaze flicking to the other ambulance.

"They're preparing to transport her to the hospital at Fort Rickman, sir."

"Not the civilian facility in Freemont?"

"She was conscious long enough to give her last name. Her husband is a sergeant on post. Sergeant Drew Davis."

Frank didn't recognize the name, but if Vivian was an army spouse, the CID would be involved in the investigation. With the Freemont police working hard on the storm-relief effort, the military might take the lead on the case.

Tonight, everyone would focus on search and rescue. By morning both the Freemont cops and the military law enforcement would have more time to question Colleen. Until then, Frank would keep her under watch.

Too many things didn't add up. In spite of being on

convalescent leave, Frank needed to learn the truth about how a military wife with a gunshot wound had ended up in Colleen's car.

Colleen tried to ignore the pointed stare of the CID agent who had dug her from the rubble. His deep-set eyes and gaunt face were troubling and cut her to the core. In fact, the only redeeming quality about the guy was his dog.

She rubbed her temple, hoping to drive away the pounding headache that had come with the storm. Her memory was fuzzy at best, and she had difficulty recalling some of the most basic information, especially pertaining to Vivian. Without thinking, she'd left her purse in her car along with the memory card.

A pickup truck pulled to a stop in the triage area. The driver, a middle-aged farmer wearing bib overalls and a baseball cap, rolled down his window and nodded to the EMT.

"We found a guy hunkered down in a ditch just over that ridge." The farmer pointed to the rise in the roadway. "His sports car was destroyed, but he survived, although he's scraped up a bit. Face could have been in worse shape if he hadn't been wearing a sweatshirt. Looks like the hood protected him. A guy with an SUV is bringing him your way."

Hooded sweatshirt. Colleen's heart jammed in her throat. Trey had a sporty BMW, although she hadn't seen which of his many cars he was driving today.

If he was the injured man, Colleen had to get out of sight. She'd come back later for the things she'd left behind.

A gold SUV headed down the hill.

Her stomach fluttered. She turned and started to walk away.

"Where are you going?" Frank called after her.

To hide.

What could she tell him? *Think. Think.*

Her stalled brain refused to work. Searching for an answer, she glanced at the house on the knoll.

"I'm taking you up on that invitation to stay with your sister." Even she heard the tremble in her voice.

Frank raised his brow. Surely he wouldn't rescind the offer?

Her pulse throbbed and sweat dampened her back.

The SUV drew closer.

Colleen waved Frank off. "Stay here and help with the rescue operation. I can find my way up the hill."

She lowered her head, wrapped her arms around her waist and started along the path with determined steps. Keeping her back to the approaching car, she was grateful for the descending twilight and the shadows cast from the tall pines. The path wound along the roadway for a short distance and then burrowed deeper into the woods.

If only she could reach the denser underbrush before the SUV got too close. She couldn't let Trey see her.

Flicking a quick glance over her shoulder, she recognized the firm set of Trey's jaw and the bulk of his shoulders as the car pulled to a stop.

No mistaking the man riding shotgun.

At that moment, he glanced up.

Ice froze her veins. Her heart slammed against her chest. If Trey recognized her, he would track her down. Not only did Colleen have incriminating photos, but she had also witnessed him shoot Vivian in cold blood.

She increased her pace and darted along the path.

"Wait, Colleen."

The military CID agent ran after her, along with his dog.

Stay away from me, she wanted to scream, but reason won out. She needed Frank. She was stranded without a car with a killer on the loose. She needed the security of his sister's house and his protection throughout the night.

Later, she'd return to the wreckage and retrieve her purse and the memory card. Tomorrow, she'd catch the bus to Atlanta. From there, she'd hop a flight for the West Coast and disappear from sight. She'd leave Trey behind along with the special agent who didn't understand what she was trying to hide.

Frank wondered at Colleen's rush to get away, but then, he wasn't the best at reading women. Case in point Audrey, who said she'd wait for him. The memory still burned like fire.

"Wait up, Colleen."

Frank ran after her. His hip ached, and his breathing was tighter than he'd like.

Before the IED, he'd never questioned his strength. Now he had to weigh everything in light of his physical stamina.

Drawing closer, he grabbed her arm.

She turned troubled eyes filled with accusation. "Let me go."

Releasing his hold, he held up both hands, palm out. "Sorry. I didn't mean to upset you."

She glanced through the bramble to the triage area, where a cluster of rescue workers gathered. "I'm still shaky."

An understatement for sure. "You've been through a lot today. The temperature's dropped since the storm. You must be cold."

"A little."

He shrugged out of his windbreaker and wrapped it around her shoulders. "This should help."

"What about you?"

"Not a problem." He pointed to the path. "Let's keep going while there's still some light."

"Are you sure your sister won't mind taking in a stray?"

He almost smiled. "She welcomed me a few weeks back with open arms. If I had to guess, I'd say she'd enjoy having another woman in the house. She claims I get a bit snarky at times."

"I'm sure she loves your company."

"She loves Duke."

Colleen almost smiled. "Who wouldn't?" She patted his head, and he wagged his tail, enjoying the attention.

"You've got brothers?" Frank asked, hoping to learn more about the reclusive flight attendant.

She faltered. Her face darkened. "One sister. She passed away four months ago."

"I'm sorry."

"So am I."

"Watch your step." Frank pointed to an area littered with rocks. Taking her arm, he supported her up the steep incline.

"Thanks," she said when they reached the top.

Stopping to catch her breath, she glanced over her shoulder. Frank followed her gaze. Darkness had settled over the small valley, but headlights from the response vehicles and flashing lights from law enforcement cut through the night.

A number of Amish buggies were on the street. Lights from additional rescue vehicles appeared in the distance.

Frank needed to get Colleen settled and then return to the triage area and wait for personnel from post to arrive.

If anything good came from the tornado, it was the wake-up call that Frank had been lingering too long, nursing his wounds. He didn't want to appear weak. Not to the military or the other CID agents. Most especially not to himself.

Colleen turned back to Evelyn's house and paused for a long moment. Perhaps she was as unsettled about moving forward as he was. Frank could relate.

But that wouldn't change the problem at hand. He needed to learn more about Colleen Brennan and the gunshot victim. Why were they on the run, and who was after them?

THREE

Some of Colleen's nervous anxiety eased when Frank opened the door to his sister's home, and she stepped inside. The dog followed.

A brick fireplace, painted white, drew her eye along with a beige couch and two side chairs, nestled around a low coffee table. An oil seascape hung over the mantel flanked by built-in shelves filled with books. She neared and glanced at the titles, seeing some of her favorites.

Frank came up behind her. "Did I tell you Evelyn is a librarian?"

"I'm in here." A voice called from the kitchen.

He motioned for Colleen to follow as he headed toward a small hallway that led to a keeping area and open kitchen.

A slender woman, early forties, with chestnut hair and big blue eyes, stood behind a granite-topped island and greeted Frank with a warm smile. She was fair and petite and contrasted with her brother's rugged frame and broad shoulders.

Colleen and her sister had shared similar facial structures, although Briana had been golden-haired like their mother, while Colleen inherited her flaming-red locks from her dad. Seeing the warmth of Evelyn's welcome made Colleen long for her own sister.

"I'm baking a ham and making potato salad for the rescue effort." She stirred mayonnaise into the bowl of boiled potatoes and sliced hard-boiled eggs.

As Colleen moved closer, Evelyn glanced up. The look on her face revealed her surprise at finding a visitor. She wiped her hand on a dish towel.

With a pronounced limp, she moved around the island and opened her arms to greet Colleen with a hug. "Welcome. Looks like you were caught in the storm."

The sincerity of Evelyn's voice touched a raw edge in the depths of Colleen's self-control. Her eyes burned and a lump formed in her throat in response to the genuine concern she heard in the older woman's voice.

Frank quickly made the introductions, his tone suddenly curt and businesslike and so opposite his sister's soothing welcome. As if unsure of where to stand or what to do next, he headed for the coffeepot.

"Care for a cup?" he asked Colleen before glancing at his sister. "Decaf, right?"

"Always at this time or I'd never sleep."

"A glass of water might be better," Colleen said. "But I don't want to trouble you."

Duke nuzzled her leg. He held a tennis ball in his mouth and wanted to play. Before she could take the ball, Frank motioned him to the corner, where he dropped the toy and obediently lay down.

"Good dog."

Frank turned to his sister. "Colleen's car was damaged by the tornado. She lives in Atlanta and hopes to return home in a few days."

"Preferably tomorrow," she quickly added.

"You need a place to spend the night." Evelyn's eyes were filled with understanding. "We have a spare room. Of course you'll stay here."

Turning to Frank, she added, "Did you bring her luggage?"

"I've got a carry-on bag in the trunk of my car, but I didn't think about it until now," Colleen admitted.

"I'll get it when I head back to the triage area," Frank volunteered.

Colleen held up her hand. "No need. I'll get it in the morning."

"Is there anyone in Atlanta you want to call who might be worried about you?" Evelyn asked.

"That's kind of you, but I have a cell phone." Colleen patted her pocket, reassured by the weight of her mobile device.

"You might not have coverage," Evelyn said. "Some of the cell towers were hit by the storm. Thankfully our landline is still working."

"I take it you got through to the rural fire department," Frank said to his sister.

She nodded. "Which was a blessing. They passed on the information to emergency personnel in town. The local radio station quoted the mayor as saying search-and-rescue operations would continue into the night and throughout the next few days."

"At a minimum." Frank glanced at his watch. "I need to hurry back."

"You need to eat something," Evelyn insisted.

He shook his head.

"Then I'll make a sandwich to take with you."

"More of your attempts to fatten me up?" His tone held a hint of levity that surprised Colleen.

Evelyn opened the refrigerator and pulled out lunch meat, cheese and mustard. As she layered the meat and cheese on two slices of bread, Frank grabbed a glass from one of the overhead cabinets. He filled it with ice and added water from the dispenser on the door of the refrigerator.

"You'll need your coat," Evelyn said, cutting the sandwich in half and wrapping it in foil.

Colleen accepted the water from Frank. From all appearances, his sister was the nurturing type, and despite the macho persona he tried to impart, the CID special agent seemed to readily accept her advice.

"I'm changing into my uniform. Fort Rickman's getting involved, and I want to help them set up."

"You're still on convalescent leave, Frank."

"Only for another week."

He glanced at Colleen and then headed into the hallway that led to the front of the house. "Back in a minute."

While Frank changed, Evelyn showed her to a guest room located behind the kitchen. "This doubles as my office and sewing room. I hope you won't mind the clutter."

A computer sat on a small desk, and colorful baskets filled with fabric and threads were neatly tucked in the shelving that covered the far wall. A double bed, nightstand and small dresser took up the rest of the space.

"If the weather warms tomorrow, you can use the screened-in porch." Colleen pointed to the French doors leading to the private sitting area. "It's usually nice this time of year, although tonight the temperature's a bit chilly."

"It's a lovely room, Evelyn, but I fear I'm putting you out."

"Nonsense. I'm glad Frank found you."

Which he had. He and Duke had found her in the rubble. If they hadn't, no telling how long she and Vivian would have been trapped.

"You're fortunate the storm spared your house," Colleen said as she glanced outside at the downed branches littering the yard.

"God answered our prayers."

Colleen nodded. "I'm sure the Amish folks prayed, as well."

"Of course. Their faith is strong. In fact, they are a resilient community and a forgiving people. They'll rebuild."

"I hate to see dreams destroyed."

Evelyn nodded knowingly. "If only we knew what the future would hold."

The melancholy in her voice gave Colleen pause. Perhaps Evelyn had her own story to tell.

"Frank said there's a bus station in Freemont."

Evelyn raised her brow. "You're in a hurry to get back to Atlanta?"

The question caught Colleen off guard. "As…as soon as possible."

Mentally weighing her options, she realized none of them were good. She couldn't fly without her driver's license and airline identification. Both were in her purse, buried in her car.

She had planned on a fast trip to Freemont to gather the last bit of evidence she needed to send Trey to jail. Now Vivian was in the hospital, and Colleen was stranded in an area devastated by a tornado. To add to her situation, she was holed up with a law enforcement officer who made her uneasy.

A tap sounded at the entrance to her room. She turned to find Frank standing in the doorway. He was clean-shaven and dressed in his army combat uniform. Maybe it was the boots he wore or the digital print of the camouflage that made him seem bigger than life.

She needed to breathe, but the air got trapped in her lungs.

"I'll be back later. Don't wait up, sis."

"The sandwich is on the counter."

"You're spoiling me." Raising his hand, he waved to Colleen and then hurried toward the kitchen.

"The sandwich," Evelyn reminded him.

"Got it," he called before the front door slammed closed behind him.

"Why don't you wash up and come back to the kitchen for something to eat." Evelyn motioned toward the hall-way.

"Thanks, but I'm not hungry."

"A bowl of soup might be good."

The woman didn't give up.

As if on cue, Colleen's stomach growled, causing her to smile. "A cup of soup sounds good."

Once Evelyn returned to the kitchen, Colleen pulled back the curtain in the bedroom and watched Frank lower the back hatch on his pickup truck. Duke hopped into the truck bed and barked as if eager to get under way.

Frank climbed behind the wheel. The sound of the engine filled the night. He turned on the headlights that flashed against the house and into the window, catching her in their glare.

She stepped away, hoping he hadn't seen her. Much as she appreciated Evelyn's hospitality and grateful though she was of having a place to stay, Colleen worried about Frank's questions and the way he stared at her when he thought she wasn't looking.

After her sister's death and her own struggle with the Atlanta police, Colleen wanted nothing more to do with law enforcement. Now she was seeking shelter in the very home of a man she should fear.

Only she didn't fear Frank. Something else stirred within her when he was near. Unease, yes, but also a feeling she couldn't identify that had her at odds with her present predicament. She needed to leave Freemont as soon as possible, but until she retrieved her purse and the photo card, she had no other choice but to stay with Frank and his sister.

Hopefully she wasn't making another mistake she would live to regret.

A desire to protect her stirred deep within Frank when he saw Colleen standing at the window as he pulled his truck out of the drive. She had a haunting beauty with her big eyes and high cheekbones and the shock of red curls that seemed unwilling to be controlled.

Did her rebellious hair provide a glimpse into who Colleen really was? She tried to maintain a quiet reserve, yet perhaps a part of her longed to be free like the strands of hair that fell in disarray around her oval face. That disparity between who Colleen tried to be and whom he had caught a glimpse of when she wasn't looking gave him pause.

Driving down the hill from his sister's house, Frank thought of his own past, and the picture he had painted for his life, all with broad brushstrokes. At one time, he'd had it all and thought the future would provide only more positive moments to share with Audrey. He found out too late that she lived life on the surface and wasn't willing to go beneath the false facade she had created.

Frank had thought she understood about sacrifice for a greater good. He'd realized his mistake when she left him, unwilling to be tied down to a wounded warrior who had to face a long, difficult recovery.

At this point, Frank didn't know who he was. Too

many things had changed that clouded the picture. He certainly wasn't the same man as the cocky, sure-of-himself CID agent patrolling an area of Afghanistan where terrorists had been seen. Perhaps he had been too confident, too caught up in his own ability to recognize the danger.

Not that he could go back or undo what had happened. He had to move forward. Donning his uniform tonight was a positive step. The stiff fabric felt good when he'd slipped into his army combat uniform.

At least he looked like a soldier, even if he wasn't sure about the future. Would he continue on with the military or put in his papers for discharge?

A decision he needed to make.

Headlights from a stream of military vehicles appeared in the distance when Frank parked at the barn. Two more ambulances from Freemont had arrived to transport the injured, and radio communication was up and running among the various search-and-rescue operations.

A fireman with wide shoulders and an equally wide neck approached Frank. "Thanks for helping with the relief effort."

"How's it look so far?"

"At least twelve Amish homes and barns have been destroyed. Close to twenty people have been identified as injured. No loss of life, but we're still looking."

"I heard Freemont had damage. A trailer park and some of the warehouses by the river."

"Might be time to clean out that entire waterfront," the fireman said, "but the mayor and town council will make that decision."

Noting the approach of the convoy, Frank pointed to a grassy area between the Amish Craft Shoppe and the collapsed barn. "Can you get someone to direct the military personnel to that level area where they can set up their operations center?"

"Will do." The fireman called two other men who used flares to direct the military vehicles into the clearing.

Frank saluted the captain who crawled from his Hummer.

"Thanks for getting here in a timely manner, sir." Frank introduced himself. "I'm CID, currently on convalescent leave, but I reside in the area and wanted to offer my assistance."

"Appreciate the help." The captain shook Frank's hand and then smiled at Duke. "Nice dog."

"He's a retired military working dog. Duke lost his sense of smell in an IED explosion, but that doesn't stop him from helping out when he can."

Frank passed on the information the fireman had shared about the damage and the injured.

"I've got engineers who will check the structural integrity of the homes still standing once we're assured all the victims have been accounted for." The captain pointed to a group of soldiers raising a tent. "We're setting up a field medical unit to help with the injured. That way the ambulances can transport those needing more extensive medical care to the hospital."

"The local fire and EMTs have a triage area you might want to check out, sir."

"Thanks for the info. I'll coordinate with them."

The captain headed for the civilian ambulances just as Special Agent Colby Voss pulled to a stop in his own private vehicle, a green Chevy.

He climbed from his car and offered Frank a warm smile along with a solid handshake. Instead of a uniform,

Colby wore slacks and a CID windbreaker. "I thought you were still on convalescent leave."

"Another week, but I'm ready to get back to work."

"Wilson will like hearing that. We're short staffed as usual, and he'd welcome another special agent."

Frank appreciated Colby's optimism. "Did anyone notify you about Vivian Davis, a gunshot victim who got caught in the storm? She's a military spouse. EMTs took her to the hospital on post."

"The call could have come in while I was away from my desk. Do you have any details?"

"Only that she flagged down a driver at a picnic park farther south, saying she needed help. A shot rang out, the woman was hit. She and the driver escaped."

"Did you question the victim?" Colby asked.

"Negative. She was slipping in and out of consciousness. EMTs needed to keep her alive."

"I'll notify CID Headquarters. What about the driver?"

"Colleen Brennan. She's a flight attendant from Atlanta. Her vehicle is buried under rubble." Frank pointed to the spot where the barn had once stood. "She won't be driving home anytime soon. My sister has a spare bedroom. I invited her to stay the night. The local police don't have time for anything except search and rescue, and I know Fort Rickman is probably equally as busy. I thought keeping an eye on her here might be a good idea, at least until we get through the next twenty-four hours or so."

"Was she injured?"

"A slight concussion and some cuts and scrapes. Nothing too serious, although she was pretty shook up and not too sure about some details. I'm hoping she'll be less confused and more willing to talk in the morning." Frank pointed to the barn. "I'm planning to check out her car if you're looking for something to do."

"Sounds good, but I've got to call Becca. She left a message on my cell after seeing video footage about the storm on the nightly news. Give me a few minutes, and I'll catch up to you."

"The last remaining portion of the barn looks like it could easily collapse, so be careful. If you've got crime scene tape, I'll cordon off the area."

"Good idea. We don't need any more injuries." Colby opened his trunk and handed the yellow roll of tape to Frank.

He grabbed a Maglite from his truck and patted his leg for Duke. "Come on, boy."

The two of them made their way to what remained of the barn. Frank heaved aside a number of boards and cleared space around the rear of Colleen's vehicle before he opened the trunk.

Aiming the Maglite, Frank saw a carry-on bag with a plastic badge identifying Colleen's airline.

"Let's check up front," he told Duke, after he had retrieved the bag and placed it on the ground.

The dog whined.

"What is it, boy?"

Duke climbed over the fallen boards and stopped at the passenger seat, where Vivian had lain earlier. Blood stained the upholstery.

"You're upset the woman was injured." Frank patted the dog's flank. "I am, too. We need to find out who shot her and why."

Bending, he felt under the seat. His fingers touched something leather. He pulled it free.

A woman's purse.

He placed it on the seat and opened the clasp. Shining the light into the side pocket, he spied Vivian's government ID card and driver's license. Tissues, face powder and high-end sunglasses lay at the bottom.

Leaning down, he again groped his hand along the floorboard. This time, his fingers curled around a smartphone. He stood and studied the mobile device.

An iPhone with all the bells and whistles.

He hit the home button. A circle with an arrow in the middle of the screen indicated a video was primed to play.

Colleen claimed to have happened upon the distressed woman, but if the two had arranged to meet, the video might have been meant for Colleen to view.

Frank hit the arrow, and the footage rolled. A man sat at a booth with Vivian sitting across from him. From the angle, the camera appeared to have been upright on the table, perhaps in a front pocket of her purse with the camera lens facing out.

The guy didn't seem to know he was being recorded.

The audio was sketchy. Frank turned up the volume.

"You brought the package?" The man's voice.

"Relax, Trey. I don't go back on my word."

Trey?

She slipped a rectangular object across the table. The man nervously glanced over his shoulder.

Frank stopped the video. His gut tightened. He'd been in law enforcement long enough to know what the small package, shrink-wrapped and vacuum sealed in plastic, probably contained.

Snow, Flake, Big C.

Also known as cocaine.

FOUR

While Evelyn busied herself in the kitchen, Colleen hurriedly ate a bowl of homemade soup and a slice of homemade bread slathered with butter.

"A friend is stopping by shortly." Evelyn wiped the counter and then rinsed the sponge in the sink. "He's a retired teacher and works with the hospitality committee at church. Ron's organizing a meal for the displaced folks and the rescue workers."

A timer dinged. She opened the oven and pulled out two green bean casseroles and a baked ham.

"The Amish want to take care of their own, but with so many homes destroyed they'll need help. Thankfully, I had a ham and fresh vegetables in the fridge, many grown by my Amish neighbors. They also baked the bread you're eating."

"It's delicious."

Finishing the last of the soup, Colleen scooted back from the table and headed to the sink. "I was hungrier than I thought. I'm sure the homeless will appreciate the food." She rinsed her dishes and silverware and loaded them in the dishwasher.

"I'd invite you to join us, but you look worn-out," Evelyn said. "Better to get a good night's sleep. There will be plenty of ways to get involved in the days ahead."

"I'm going back to Atlanta."

Evelyn nodded. "That's right. I didn't mean to change your plans, but if you decide to stay longer, you know you're welcome."

A knock sounded. She hurried to open the front door and invited a man inside. Returning to the kitchen, she introduced Ron Malone. He was of medium build and height but had expressive eyes and a warm smile, especially when he looked at Evelyn.

For an instant, Colleen had a sense of déjà vu.

Shaking it off, she tried to focus on what Evelyn was saying. Something about organizing the food.

"Colleen was driving through the area when the tornado hit," Evelyn explained. "Her car was damaged. She hopes to get back to Atlanta in a day or two."

Tomorrow.

"I'm amazed at the immediate response from so many who want to help." Colleen shook Ron's outstretched hand. "I doubt the same would happen in Atlanta."

"I think you'd be surprised about the number of caring people even in the city."

Colleen didn't share his opinion, but Evelyn's friend had an engaging manner, and from the way Evelyn was smiling, she must think so, as well.

"If you don't mind, I'll say good-night and head to my room."

Evelyn gave her a quick hug. "Hope you sleep well."

Colleen didn't plan to sleep. She planned to do something else, something she didn't want Evelyn to know about.

Timing would be important. She needed to be back at the house before Frank came home. He was the last person she wanted to see tonight.

Once the front door closed and Ron had backed out of

the driveway, Colleen left the house through the French doors and scurried across the yard to the path in the woods. Gingerly, she picked her way down the hill.

A large military tent had been erected since she'd left the triage area. It was located close to the Amish Craft Shoppe and well away from the barn.

Staying in the shadows, she inched forward, grateful that her eyes had adjusted to the darkness. All along Amish Road, flashing lights illuminated the ongoing rescue effort.

Glancing back, she saw the glow in Evelyn's kitchen window like a beacon of hope in the midst of the destruction. The sincere welcome and concern she had read in her hostess's gaze had brought comfort.

If only she could sense a bit of welcome from Frank. He revealed little except a mix of fatigue and frustration. The only time she'd seen his expression brighten was when he'd talked to his sister. Other than that, he'd seemed closed, as if holding himself in check.

Judging by his appearance, he must have either been sick or sustained an injury. Her heart softened for an instant before she caught herself and reeled in her emotions. She didn't want to delve into his past or any pain he carried. She had enough of her own.

Her eyes burned as she thought of her sister. Too often, Briana had called begging for money to buy more drugs. Colleen had adopted a tough-love attitude that had backfired. She had hoped going after Trey would ease the burden of guilt that weighed her down. Now Vivian was injured, and the evidence she had planned to give Colleen was buried in the rubble.

Squinting into the night, Colleen saw the outline of her Honda, partially covered with debris. The passenger door was still open. Using her cell phone for light, she approached the car and leaned inside.

Working her hand across the floorboard, she searched for two purses, one of which contained the evidence Vivian had promised. The other—her own handbag—held the tiny memory card filled with digital photos.

Trying to recall the series of events when she pulled into the roadside park, Colleen bent lower. Vivian had dropped her purse at her feet as soon as she'd climbed into the car. Colleen extended her arm under the seat and then stretched down even farther.

A hand touched her shoulder.

She jerked. Her head knocked against the console, hitting near the spot injured earlier in the storm. The pain made her gasp for air. Rubbing the initial knot that was still noticeable, she turned to stare into Frank's dark eyes.

"Looking for something?" His voice was laced with accusation.

"My...my carry-on bag," she stammered.

He gripped her upper arm and pulled her from the car.

"What are you doing?" Her voice cracked, making her sound like a petulant child when she wanted to be forceful and self-assured.

"Let go of my arm," she demanded, more satisfied with the intensity of her command.

"Promise me you won't run."

She straightened her back. As if she could outrun Frank.

"I was searching for *my own* luggage in *my own* car. That doesn't warrant being manhandled."

His head tilted. He released his hold on her.

She rubbed her arm. He hadn't hurt her, but he had been aggressive.

Dark shadows played over his steely gaze. "What were you really looking for, Colleen?"

Refusing to be intimidated, she held her ground. "I just told you. My carry-on."

"Which I found in the trunk of your car." He held up the shoulder bag Vivian had carried. "Was this what you wanted?"

"That's Vivian's purse. She dropped it on the floor when she slipped into the car."

"Then maybe you were looking for her cell." He held up the iPhone.

"Should I have been?"

He leaned closer. "You tell me."

"Look, Frank, we're not getting anywhere fast. I'm sure Vivian would like her purse and phone back. As for me, I'm not interested in either item."

"Did Vivian tell you about the video? The near-field communication function was turned on. Had she planned to send a copy of the video to your phone?"

"I don't know anything about a video."

Vivian had evidence she'd wanted to share. A chill ran down Colleen's spine. Frank had found what Vivian had promised to provide.

He tapped Vivian's phone. A picture appeared on the screen of a rectangular object wrapped in plastic.

Colleen leaned in to view the screen. "What's in the shrink wrap?"

"Don't play dumb. You know exactly what the package contains."

She pulled back, frustrated by the hostility in his voice.

When she didn't respond, he took a step closer, too close.

"Coke. Crack. Crystal." He glared down at her. "You get the message?"

His eyes narrowed even more. "Were you and Vivian working for the guy in the video, only maybe Vivian was dealing on the side? Maybe she wanted to rip him off? He got angry and followed her."

Frank hesitated for half a heartbeat. "Or was he following you? Did you and Vivian plan to blackmail him? Maybe you wanted payment for the video. Did you ask for cash, or did you want the payoff in drugs?"

Anger swelled within her. Frank was just like the cops in Atlanta.

"Do you always jump to the wrong conclusion?" she threw back at him. "Must not bode well for your law enforcement career."

Fire flashed from his eyes. She had struck a sore spot. He took a step back and pursed his lips.

"We need to talk." He glanced up the hill. "At Evelyn's house."

"You mean you're not going to haul me off to jail?"

"Tell me the truth, Colleen. That's all I want. Why did you meet Vivian at the roadside park? Who's the guy in the video? Was he the shooter? If so, why'd he come after you? If you'll answer those questions, then I'll listen. If you're unwilling, I'll transport you to CID Headquarters tonight."

She raised her chin with determination and stood her ground. "I'm not military. You don't have jurisdiction over me."

A muscle in his neck twitched. "Then I'll contact the local authorities."

"They're busy, tied up with the aftermath of the storm. I doubt they'd be interested."

"You're wrong. A woman was shot. She was in a video

and appears to have been dealing drugs. The local authorities may be busy, but they're not that busy."

Colleen breathed out a deep sigh of resignation. She didn't have a choice. "You're right, Frank. We need to talk."

"I've got my truck." He pointed to where it was parked on the far side of the Amish store.

If only she had noticed the vehicle earlier. She would have turned around and returned to Evelyn's house and not attempted to search her car while Frank was in the area.

Hindsight wouldn't help her now.

She walked purposefully toward the pickup with Frank following close behind.

Duke stared at her from inside the cab. Frank reached around her and opened the passenger door. "Down, boy."

The dog jumped onto the gravel driveway. Colleen slipped into the passenger seat.

Once Duke was secured in the back of the pickup, Frank returned to the barn and stretched crime scene tape around her car. Her heart skittered in her chest. The yellow tape made everything that had happened today even more real. She raked fingers through her thick curls. What had she been thinking, trying to cover up information from the authorities?

Her eyes burned. She clenched her fists, blinking back the tears. She needed to be strong. If she broke down, Frank would think she had something to hide.

Walking back to his truck, he raised his cell phone to his ear. Was he answering a call or making one? To local law enforcement perhaps?

Would the police be waiting for her at Evelyn's house? She bit her lip and looked into the darkness. How had she gotten into this predicament when all she wanted was to talk sense into Vivian and gather more evidence against Trey?

Frank rounded the car and slid into the driver's seat. His long, lean body hardly fit in the confined space. She tried to imagine him bulked up. Perhaps he wouldn't seem as menacing then. Somehow his pensive expression and hollowed cheeks gave him a frosty appearance that was less than approachable.

He turned the key in the ignition. Colleen was glad for the rumble of the engine and the sound of the wheels on the gravel drive as he backed away from the Amish store.

She didn't want to talk to Frank, yet that's what would happen shortly. Colleen wouldn't lie, but she couldn't tell him everything. He'd be like the other law enforcement officers she had approached.

They hadn't believed her.

Frank wouldn't believe her either.

Instead of driving up the mountain, Frank headed to where the rescue crews were working farther south along Amish Road.

Colleen didn't question the change of direction. Instead she gazed out the passenger window as if distancing herself from Frank.

Through the rearview mirror, he saw Duke balanced in the truck bed, his nose sniffing the wind. The dog had an innate ability to read people. Duke had taken to Colleen from the onset, yet Frank wouldn't make a judgment about Colleen based on his canine's desire for attention.

Nearing the rescue activity, he pulled to the side of the road and cut the engine. "I'll just be a minute."

She nodded but didn't question the stop.

Duke whined to get down.

"Stay and guard the truck." *Guard Colleen, as well.*

Huge generators operated the emergency lights and rumbled in the night. Frank's eyes adjusted to the brightness, and he quickly searched for a familiar face in the wash of rescue personnel.

Spying Colby near one of the medical vehicles, Frank hurried forward. The other agent held up both hands and shrugged with regret.

"Frank, I'm sorry. I got caught up in a problem with the Amish and never made it to the barn. Did you find what you were looking for?"

"I found Colleen." Frank glanced back at the truck. She held her head high and stared straight ahead. If only he could tap into that defensive shell she wore as protection.

He turned back to Colby. "Any chance you can spare an hour or two?"

"We're in good shape here. What do you need?"

"Colleen was rummaging through her car. Supposedly she was searching for her carry-on bag. Earlier I had found Vivian's phone with a video showing what appeared to be a drug exchange."

"You know we're not allowed to search a suspect's cell phone without a warrant."

Frank nodded. "I was checking to see if it still had power. The video came up on the screen. I didn't have to search for anything, and I didn't access her call log, much as I would have liked that information, as well."

"You think both women were dealing?"

"I'm not sure what to think, but Colleen's ready to answer questions, and I want you there since I'm not officially on duty."

"You could take her into post."

Frank nodded. "That's an option, but Fort Rickman's digging out from the storm. I doubt anyone wants to stop that effort to question a witness when we can handle it here."

"Good point. I'd be glad to serve as another set of eyes and ears. Give me a minute to let the captain know that I'll be away from the area for a bit. I'll meet you at Evelyn's house."

Frank appreciated having another CID agent present when he questioned Colleen. She seemed legit, but even pretty young things with red hair popped pills and dealt drugs. Better to be cautious instead of making another mistake. Frank hadn't seen Audrey for who she really was. He needed to be right about Colleen.

Was she a deceptive drug dealer or an innocent woman caught in the wrong place at the wrong time?

FIVE

Knowing Frank would be thorough with his questioning, Colleen climbed from his truck as soon as they got back to Evelyn's house. While he tended to his dog, she headed for the kitchen. Working quickly, she filled the coffee basket with grounds and poured water into the canister. The rich brew would help her see things more clearly, and the caffeine would ease her fatigue.

The scent of coffee soon filled the kitchen. She pulled mugs from the cabinet and placed them on the counter. Frank entered the house and wiped his feet on the rug by the door before heading down the hallway.

Just as she expected, his gaze was filled with questions when he stepped into the kitchen.

"The coffee will be ready in a minute," she said, hoping to deflect his initial frustration.

"Are you and Vivian dealing drugs?" he asked without preamble.

"Of course not."

"A woman was shot and fell into your car. Your rear window took a hit, which means you could have been a target, yet you didn't know who the assailant was or why he was after Vivian. You didn't even claim to know her name until you inadvertently shared that information when she was fighting for her life."

Colleen bit her lip, not knowing what she should tell him and where she should start.

Frank continued to stare at her. "You know a lot more than you let on, Colleen. The video shows Vivian dealing drugs. She was injured in your car. Looks to me like you're involved. The CID will investigate, as will the local police. It's time to start talking."

Trembling internally, Colleen struggled to appear calm and in control. Thankfully, her hand didn't shake when she poured coffee and handed the filled mug to the man who had followed Frank into the kitchen.

He wore a CID windbreaker and had watched the exchange with a raised brow. The guy was shorter than Frank but carried an additional ten to twenty pounds—all muscle.

"I'm Colleen Brennan," she stated matter-of-factly. "And you are?"

"Colby Voss. Special agent, Criminal Investigation Division."

"From Fort Rickman?"

He nodded.

"Then you work with Frank," she added, following the logical progression.

"Not yet. He's on convalescent leave and will be assigned to the post CID when he goes back on active duty."

She turned to Frank. "So you're not officially on duty."

"My leave status doesn't change the fact that I'm a CID agent. We still need to talk." His gaze was chilling. He wanted answers, not random chatter.

"It's time for you to come clean, Colleen."

She nodded. After filling a cup for Frank and one for herself, she carried both of them to the kitchen table. "I'm sure you're as tired as I am. Let's sit while we talk."

He groaned with frustration, but pulled out a chair

across from her and lowered himself into the seat. Grabbing the coffee mug, he took a sip.

Colby sat at the end of the table and retrieved a small tablet and pen from his pocket. "I'll make note of anything you want to share, ma'am."

"Thank you." She tried to smile. "You're investigating Vivian's shooting?"

The agent tapped his pen and then raised his gaze to meet Frank's. "Special Agent in Charge Wilson will make that call. Right now, I'm here with Frank to help with the local recovery effort."

She nodded and then hesitated, trying to determine where to begin. "At seventeen, my sister, Briana, ran away from home to marry a shiftless bum named Larry Kelsey. He promised her a lot of things, including an acting career in Hollywood. The marriage didn't last long. She got rid of Larry, but kept her dream of fame and fortune."

Colleen tried to smile. "In spite of Briana's skewed sense of what was important in life and her naïveté, she was beautiful and poised and articulate."

Everything Colleen wasn't.

"About a year after her divorce, she took up with an Atlanta photographer. Although somewhat successful, the photography business was a front for his drug-trafficking operation. He got Briana hooked and then used her as a mule to bring in drugs from Colombia. Four months ago, she overdosed from drugs he'd given her and died."

Colby shifted in his seat as he took down the information. Frank steeled his jaw and continued to stare at Colleen as she continued.

"One day, I…I ran into Trey in the grocery store." She played her finger around the rim of her mug. She wanted to laugh at the irony, but everything caught in her throat.

"Our shopping carts collided, which he thought was accidental. He didn't realize I'd been watching him and had planned our meeting. Trey was apologetic and a perfect gentleman, or so he tried to seem. Because of Briana's married name, he never realized I was her sister."

"Trey's last name?" Colby asked.

"Trey Howard," she replied. "I let him take me out a few times. Nice places. Upscale eateries. Plays at the Fox, art shows at the High Museum. He said we liked the same things. At least that's what he thought." Again she hesitated.

"So you had a relationship," Frank pressed, his tone as hard as his gaze.

She held up her hand in protest. "If you're implying that we were involved or that anything happened between us, you've got it all wrong. As I kept telling Trey, we were friends, enjoying time together."

When she took a sip of coffee, Colby added, "But things changed."

"I'm a flight attendant with some seniority. I fly to Colombia two or three times a month. Trey mentioned having worked there on a resort property. He took photos for a brochure and pamphlets for vacationers looking for a new place to visit. The photos he showed me were lovely. He told me he'd arrange for me to enjoy an all-expenses-paid stay there on my next layover. The resort liked airline personnel and would be happy to have me as their guest at no expense to me."

"You took him up on the offer?" Frank asked.

"I made an excuse, but the next time I was scheduled to fly, he mentioned it again. He thought I didn't want to be beholden to anyone. He needed a package brought back into the US and suggested I do him the favor in return for the resort accommodations."

Frank leaned in closer. "Did you ask what was in the package?"

"No, but I didn't need a degree in law enforcement to know the package probably contained something the government might not want brought into this country."

"You notified the authorities?"

She pulled in a deep breath. "Trey was well connected. I needed evidence before I accused him of anything illegal."

"Go on," Frank encouraged.

"One night I surprised him at his condo. He was working in his office, but said he needed to take a break and was glad I had stopped by. We were in the living area when he got a phone call. He apologized for taking the call and said he'd be tied up for ten to fifteen minutes. I excused myself to use the restroom. His office was across the hall, but he didn't go there to talk. Instead, he went outside on the deck, which gave me the opportunity I'd been hoping for."

"You searched his office?" Frank seemed surprised.

"I had questions that needed answers and wanted to be sure I was right about who Trey really was."

"You put yourself in danger, Colleen."

"Maybe, but Trey trusted me at that point. Besides—" she raised her brow "—I'm sure you've been in harm's way a time or two."

"It's my job. You're a civilian and not law enforcement."

"That's correct, but if the authorities weren't interested in bringing down a known drug trafficker, I had to get involved."

At the time, she hadn't thought about the danger to herself. She'd thought only of gathering the evidence she needed.

"Give me all the information you have about Trey," Colby interjected.

She provided his address and phone number. "He's got a studio in College Park, not far from the airport, and another one in Midtown."

"What did you find that night?" Frank asked.

"A list of names that included two young women I'd read about in the *Atlanta Journal-Constitution* some weeks earlier. Jackie Leonard and Patty Owens."

Colby wrote the names in his notebook.

"Both women had disappeared months earlier. They worked in the King's Club downtown. Jackie's body was found stuffed in the locked trunk of an automobile in long-term parking at the airport. The car had been stolen. Patty's body was recovered in a shallow grave in Union City, south of the airport."

"Had you known the women?" Frank asked.

She shook her head. "I told you, I read about them in the *AJC*, but their stories aren't much different from Briana's. I'm sure Trey promised them payment in drugs if they brought a few packages into the country for him."

"Finding their names on a list doesn't establish the photographer's guilt."

"Maybe not, but it does increase the cloud of suspicion hanging over his head."

Frank pursed his lips. "Let's go back to when you were in Trey's office. You saw a list of names and recognized the two women in question."

"That's right." She nodded.

"Did you find anything else?"

"Trey said he'd been working, so I clicked on his computer. A photo appeared on the screen."

Colby glanced up.

"Go on," Frank prompted.

"The picture showed a table near a huge window that looked down on a swimming pool and lush gardens with the ocean in the distance. Bricks wrapped in plastic were on the table."

"Shrink-wrapped in plastic?"

She nodded.

Frank's tone hardened. "Just like the package Vivian handed off in the video."

Colleen raked her hand through her hair and sighed. "Yes."

Colby sniffed. "Seems I missed something."

Frank pulled the iPhone from his pocket and hit the home button, then the play arrow. He held it up for Colleen to see. "Who's the guy in the footage?"

She leaned across the table. "Trey Howard."

"That's what I thought." Frank handed the cell to Colby. "As I mentioned earlier, Vivian had the near-field communication function turned on."

"Because she planned to copy the video to someone else's phone." Colby made a notation in his tablet.

Frank turned back to Colleen. "How'd you hook up with Vivian?"

"Her name was on the list, along with a phone number. I recognized the Georgia area code, and did a search on the internet."

She glanced at Colby. "Vivian likes social media. I learned her husband was deployed to Afghanistan, and she was interested in modeling so she'd had photographs taken for her portfolio."

"Trey did the photography?" Frank asked.

"That's right. He can be charming when he wants something. I'm sure he told Vivian she'd be a successful cover model."

"But he wasn't interested in her career."

"Hardly." She pulled in a breath. "Trey needed another mule to transport drugs into the country."

"How can you be certain?"

"I called her. She was scared. Her husband had redeployed home, and she wanted to cut off all contact with Trey."

Frank shook his head and narrowed his gaze. His tone was laced with skepticism. "She admitted to bringing a package into the US from Colombia?"

"Not in so many words, but I understood what she was trying to tell me."

"Why would she reveal anything over the phone?"

"I knew enough about Trey and how he operated to convince her. Plus, she'd met Briana at Trey's photo studio the day she was having her portfolio done."

"Wasn't Trey afraid the girls he used would rat him out to the cops?"

"I don't know how Trey's mind functions, but he's despicable and conniving, and he kept close tabs on anyone who worked for him. If they talked about leaving his operation, he got rid of them."

"Do you know that for sure?"

She sighed. "I don't have proof. I do have what you'd call circumstantial evidence that points to him."

"You think Trey killed Jackie Leonard and Patty Owens?"

"Maybe not personally, but he could have ordered one of the thugs who are part of his operation to do his dirty work."

"Could have?" Frank repeated the phrase she had used. "Did Trey kill your sister?"

"She overdosed on drugs he provided."

"You notified the authorities?"

"I did, but they had other, more pressing cases to investigate. Or so it seemed."

"Did Briana tell you about Trey?"

"She…she was slipping into a coma and died soon after I got to the ER. The only thing she said was to stop Trey Howard."

Which Colleen had vowed to do.

Had she made a mistake by taking on so much by herself? She rubbed her forehead and swallowed the lump that clogged her throat. She wanted to cry, but she couldn't appear weak. Not with Frank sitting across the table.

He scooted out of his chair and reached for the coffee carafe. He refilled her cup and his.

Colby held up his hand. "No more for me."

"Let's go back to Vivian," Frank said when he returned to the table. "You two decided to meet?"

"That's right. At the roadside park, but Trey was hiding in the woods."

"Why risk meeting her?"

"Vivian said she had something that would prove his guilt. I wanted that evidence."

"Evidence or drugs?"

Colleen didn't know whether to burst into tears or pound her fist on the table at his pigheadedness. She did neither. Instead she willed her expression to remain neutral and her voice controlled.

"I planned to mail whatever evidence Vivian provided, along with the list of names and the photo I found on Trey's computer, to the DEA."

"You have the photo?"

"I used the camera on my phone and took a snapshot of his computer screen. It's not the best quality, but I thought it was enough to get the police interested."

"If it's still on your phone, send the photo to my email," Frank requested.

"I'll need a copy," Colby added. Both men provided their online addresses. Colleen plugged the information into her phone and sent the photo as an attachment.

Frank left the kitchen and returned with his laptop in hand. He placed it on the table, hit the power button and quickly accessed his inbox. After opening the attachment Colleen had sent, he enhanced the screen.

"There's some type of case on the edge of the table with an identity tag, although it's too blurred to read."

She nodded. "The tag says Howard. It's Trey's camera case. That's why I thought the cop would be interested."

"But he wasn't?"

"He said I could have pulled the photo off the internet."

Colby glanced at the computer screen over Frank's shoulder. "Any idea where the picture was taken?"

"In La Porta Verde, the Colombian resort Trey wanted me to visit. As I mentioned, Trey had done the photo layout for their brochures and website when the resort was first built."

Frank tapped in the name of the resort. The home page appeared. He hit Additional Photos and clicked through a series of still shots. "Here it is. The same pool and gardens with the ocean as a backdrop."

Although still not satisfied with the direction of the questioning, Colleen felt somewhat relieved that Frank and Colby recognized the connection between the photo from Trey's laptop and the resort website.

"I sent the website URL to the Atlanta police," she continued, "along with the photo. The officer who talked to me didn't see the tie-in and said neither seemed relevant to him."

"Who'd you deal with?"

"An officer named Anderson."

Colby returned to the table and made note of the name. "Did he want to talk to you in person?"

She shook her head.

"So your only dealing with the police was over the phone to a cop named Anderson?" Frank asked.

"I dealt with two different officers at two different times. After Briana died, I contacted a cop named Sutherland. He worked close to where she lived." Colleen glanced down at her partially filled mug, remembering the less than desirable area. "He was a tough guy who didn't seem interested in the fact that she'd OD'd. He kept asking pointed questions about my relationship with my sister and insinuated I had something to do with her death."

Frank shook his head. "That doesn't make sense."

Colleen bristled. "Maybe not, but I'm just telling you what happened."

Seeing the frustration plainly written on Frank's face, she glanced down and rubbed her hand over the table. "The cop talked about the free flow of drugs to the inner city often brought in by dealers who lived in the nicer neighborhoods."

"Did you mention the photographer's name?"

She shook her head. "Sutherland made it perfectly clear that he wasn't interested in the accusations of a dying addict."

"What about Anderson? Did you have any more contact with him?"

"Not face-to-face, but someone came to my apartment."

Frank glanced at Colby then back at her. "Go on."

"I had a short overnight flight. The gal who lives in

the apartment across the hall called to tell me someone had been looking for me."

"Anderson?"

"I'm not sure. He wasn't in uniform, but Trey had boasted of having connections with the Atlanta PD. I was afraid Anderson might be on the take."

"Why would you jump to that conclusion?"

She shrugged. "Call it woman's intuition, but a warning bell went off. I had my carry-on bag so I checked into a motel instead of going home."

"That's when you contacted Vivian."

"A few days later. I needed more evidence, which I planned to mail to the DEA."

"Calling them on the phone would be a whole lot easier."

"Vivian didn't want her name used, and I didn't want the call traced back to me."

"Because?" Frank asked.

"I didn't know if they'd believe me."

She stared across the table at Frank, who seemed like the other cops with whom she'd dealt. "You don't believe me either."

He hesitated for a long moment. "I'm not sure what I believe."

His words cut her to the quick.

She glanced at Colby. "What about you?"

"I'm just making note of your statement, ma'am. More information will be needed before I can satisfactorily evaluate your response."

"Lots of words to say you're not on my side." She shoved her chair away from the table. "Neither of you are."

Standing, she glared at Frank. "If you'll excuse me.

I'll answer any additional questions you might have in the morning."

She turned on her heel and walked with determined steps to the guest room. Closing the door behind her, she dropped her head in her hands and cried.

Frank let her go. She was worn-out and on the brink of shattering. He felt as frustrated as she looked and needed time to process what she had already revealed. Parts of her story seemed valid, although her attempt to bring down a drug dealer single-handedly was hard to accept. Yet surely she could have made up a more plausible story—and one that was less convoluted—if she was trying to cover up her own involvement.

He turned back to his laptop. "Let's check out those newspaper articles about Jackie Leonard and Patty Owens."

Searching through the *AJC* archives, Frank located information on both women. Just as Colleen had said, the girls had worked at the King's Club in Atlanta. Frank checked the address and mentioned the location to Colby.

He nodded. "The heart of the inner city. Crime is rampant in that area. Those girls were flirting with trouble"

"Looks like they found it." Frank read the news stories about their bodies being found. "Know anyone in the Atlanta PD?"

"There used to be a guy. Former military. George Ulster. I could see if he's still there."

"Find out if he knows Sutherland or Anderson. Get his take on both guys. See if anyone suspects either of them is dirty. Then see what Ulster knows about the two women and whether the PD has any leads. Mention Colleen's sister, just in case there's a tie-in. Seems all three women were on a downward spiral." Frank shook his head with regret. "And hit bottom."

The front door opened, and Evelyn's laughter filtered down the hallway. Stepping into the kitchen, her face sobered. She glanced first at Frank, who quickly logged out of the archives, and then nodded to Colby.

Ron walked up behind her. "Evening, folks."

To her credit, Evelyn seemed to realize this wasn't the time for late-night chatter. She patted his arm. "It's late, Ron. We need to say good-night."

She hurried him toward the door. After a hasty few words, he left the house, and Evelyn headed to her room.

Frank closed his laptop and stood. The energy had drained from him. He grabbed the mugs off the table and placed them in the dishwasher.

Colby glanced at his watch. "It's late. I need to get back to post. I'll take the iPhone with me and stop by headquarters in the morning. Hopefully, I'll be able to talk to Wilson about getting a warrant to access her call list."

"The Freemont police need to be in the loop, but I want Wilson's approval before I do anything."

Colby headed for the hallway and then turned back. "Try to get some sleep, Frank. She's not going anywhere. At least not tonight. Besides, we all might think a bit more clearly in the morning."

Frank watched his friend leave the house. He planned to lock the doors and let Duke have the run of the house. If anyone tried to get in or out, the dog would sound a warning. Frank needed to be careful and cautious. He didn't want anything to happen to Colleen, whether she was telling the truth or not.

SIX

Colleen woke the next morning with a pounding headache. She touched the lump on her forehead and groaned, thinking back over everything that had happened.

Vivian! God, help her. Heal her.

If only she could get an update on the army wife's condition. As soon as Vivian was able to talk, the police and military authorities would question her. The video proved she had been working for Trey. Even if she claimed innocence, Vivian had brought drugs into the United States from Colombia and would, no doubt, be tried and prosecuted.

Would her guilt rub off on Colleen?

Throwing her legs over the side of the bed, she sat up and groaned again. How had her once orderly, controlled life gotten so out of hand? She longed to flee Freemont and Georgia and wipe everything she knew about Trey and his trafficking from her memory. As if she could.

Thinking back over Frank's barrage of questions last night, she sighed. She had kept some information from Frank, not wanting to fuel the flame of his disbelief. Still, she should have mentioned seeing Trey at the triage area right after the twister hit.

How could she have been so forgetful? Actually more like stupid. Probably because of her own nervousness and because Frank's penetrating gaze had left her frazzled and totally undone.

She specifically hadn't mentioned the memory card because of the digital photo she feared Frank might see. A photo taken of her with Trey's so-called friends, who were probably involved in his drug operation.

Frank didn't believe her now, and she refused to give him any more reason to doubt her. His cryptic and caustic tone had been hard enough to deal with last night. As much as she didn't want to face him in the light of day, he needed to know Trey could still be in the area.

Leaving the comfort of the bed, she walked to the window and opened the shades. Her mood plummeted as low as the gray cloud cover that blocked the sun and put a heavy pall on the day. At least it wasn't raining.

Needing something to hold on to, she once again reviewed the steps she needed to take to get out of Freemont. Once she retrieved her identification and the memory card, she would head back to Atlanta. Catching a flight to the West Coast seemed her best option. As Frank had suggested last night, she could notify the Atlanta DEA by phone—an untraceable cell—or even by email, all the while staying out of the agency's radar and away from Trey Howard and the men who worked for him.

A safer escape plan might be to drive to Birmingham, two hours west in Alabama, and fly out of that airport. If Trey's men or the Atlanta PD were checking Hartsfield, she didn't want to walk into a trap after all her hard work trying to prove Trey's guilt.

Had he already returned to Atlanta?

Or was he still in Freemont?

If so, it was because he was looking for her. Knowing

how effective Trey was in getting what he wanted, she couldn't successfully hide out for long.

With a shudder, she yanked the curtain closed again and hastily slipped into jeans and a lightweight sweater from her carry-on bag.

Colleen looked at her reflection in the mirror after she'd brushed her teeth and scrubbed her face in the adjoining bathroom. Her cheeks were flushed from the abrasive washcloth she'd scrubbed with and the cold water she'd splashed on her face.

Running a comb through her hair, she hoped to untangle the mess of curls that swirled around her face. She usually relied on the products she'd forgotten to pack to tame her unruly mane.

All she could do was roll her eyes at the halo of locks that circled her face. She'd never liked her red hair, and this morning's frizz made her look like Little Orphan Annie, only older and in no way cute or endearing.

For a fleeting moment, Colleen wondered what type of woman Frank liked. Blondes, perhaps, with rosy cheeks and finely arched brows. Maybe jet-black hair and ivory skin turned his fancy. Or women with big eyes and tiny, bow-shaped mouths.

She scoffed at her foolishness. Why would she even consider such thoughts? As far as she'd seen, the CID agent was all business with no pleasure allowed.

Colleen made the bed and tidied the room. After ensuring the colorful quilt and lace pillow shams were in place, she let out a deep breath and opened the door to the hallway.

The smell of fried eggs and bacon, mixed with the rich aroma of fresh-brewed coffee, led her to the kitchen. Usually Colleen skipped breakfast, but this morning her stomach growled with hunger, and her mouth watered for whatever Evelyn was cooking.

Stepping into the airy room, she was greeted with a wide smile from her hostess. Standing at the counter, Evelyn was arranging biscuits, still warm from the oven, in a cloth-lined basket.

"Tell me all the food I smell isn't just for you and Frank," Colleen said with a laugh.

"Help yourself. I've got four egg-and-bacon casseroles in the oven for the rescue workers. Ron's coming over at nine-thirty to take them to the triage area. You're welcome to join us if you feel able, but first, you need breakfast."

"Coffee sounds good. Mind if I pour a cup?"

"Mugs are in the cabinet closest to the stove."

Colleen selected a sturdy mug with a blue design. "Polish pottery, isn't it?"

Evelyn nodded. "Frank gave me the set for my birthday two years ago. They're popular with the military."

Colleen enjoyed the weight of the pottery as she filled it with coffee.

"Cream's in the refrigerator. There's sugar on the counter."

"Black works for me."

"You're like Frank. He claims sugar spoils the taste."

Colleen tried to seem nonchalant as she took a sip of the hot brew and then asked, "Is Frank helping with the relief effort?"

"He's in his room getting ready. I tried to convince him to sleep in this morning. I heard him pacing until the wee hours. In case you haven't noticed, my brother has a mind of his own, which sometimes causes him problems. He thinks he can do the things he used to do before his surgery."

"I heard mention of convalescent leave last night. Was Frank wounded during a deployment?"

Evelyn nodded. "He entered a building while on patrol in Afghanistan. An IED exploded and trapped him in the rubble. Duke found him and alerted the rescuers who pulled him to safety the next day."

"No wonder dog and master are so close."

"Inseparable is more like it."

"They make a good team."

"Speaking of teams, Ron needs help with the breakfast line this morning. Are you interested?"

"Count me in."

A bedroom door closed, and footsteps sounded in the hallway. Colleen tightened her grip on the mug, unsure how to react when she saw Frank.

He nodded as he entered the kitchen, looking rested and self-assured. "Morning, ladies."

"Do you have time for breakfast?" Evelyn seemed unaware of the tension Colleen felt.

"Not today." He glanced at his watch, equally oblivious to her unease. "When do you expect Ron?"

"Soon."

"Tell him folks have been notified that food will be available in the triage area. The volunteers will arrive first, followed by Amish families."

"I'll let him know."

Frank glanced at Colleen. "Can you lend a hand?"

"Of course, if Ron needs help."

"I'm sure he will." Frank stared at her a moment longer than necessary, causing her heart to flutter, but not in a good way.

She kept remembering his pointed questions from the night before.

"Then I'll see you shortly." With another nod, he hurried outside along with Duke.

He had backed his truck out the driveway before Colleen could shake off the nervous edge that hit as soon as Frank had stepped into the kitchen. If only she could react to his nearness in a less unsettling way. He seemed like a good man, but Frank was a CID agent first, and he was convinced she had some part in the drug operation.

"What would you like for breakfast?" Evelyn asked, interrupting her thoughts.

Colleen smiled. "I'd love a slice of the homemade bread you served with the soup last night."

"That's easy enough. Toasted with butter and jelly?"

"You're spoiling me."

A knock at the door had Evelyn tugging her hair into place and glancing at her reflection as she passed the mirror in the hallway.

"You look lovely," Colleen assured her and was rewarded with a backward wave of hand as Evelyn hurried to open the door.

Ron stepped inside and followed her into the kitchen, where he greeted Colleen and then began carrying the casseroles out to his car.

Colleen downed her coffee, forsaking the toast she didn't have time to fix or eat, and then grabbed the bowl of fresh fruit from the counter and hastened outside.

She stopped short on the front porch. Her heart skipped a beat as she stared at the SUV parked in the driveway.

A gold SUV.

Ron started down the sidewalk toward her.

She'd had a sense of déjà vu when Evelyn introduced them last night. No wonder.

Ron was the driver who had transported Trey to the triage area.

* * *

The temperature had risen slightly, but the day was overcast and about as gloomy as Frank's mood. The military had erected a flagpole near the triage area, and the American flag flapped in the breeze that blew from the west.

Allen Quincy was spearheading the Freemont rescue effort. Midfifties with silver hair and bushy brows, the mayor quickly briefed Frank about the rescue operation.

The engineer from Fort Rickman had checked the houses that had remained standing. A handful of the structures needed to be shored up before they'd be safe enough for the families to occupy. The army was offering manpower and supplies to any of the Amish willing to accept the help.

Earlier this morning, Colby had met with Bishop Zimmerman and eased the Amish leader's concerns about accepting the outreach. Once he realized the aid was freely given and in no way meant that his community was beholden to the military, he willingly accepted the help.

With civilian and military personnel working together, the rescue and reconstruction was progressing, but people were still without homes and many had been hospitalized.

Colby pulled to a stop in front of the tent where medical triage and evaluations were being done and waited until Frank finished talking to the mayor.

"How 'bout some coffee?" Colby called from his car, holding up two paper cups.

Frank smiled and reached through the open window to accept Colby's offer. "You must have read my mind."

"My body needed caffeine. I thought you might feel the same, especially after the late night."

"Thanks for listening to Colleen and passing the information on to the chief."

Colby held up his hand. "I didn't get Wilson. He was tied up with the general, but he sent a message through Sergeant Raynard Otis. Wilson wants to see you. Ray will call and set up an appointment."

"When?"

"Probably when post gets back to normal."

"A couple days or so?"

"That sounds about right." Colby sipped the coffee.

"I'm sure Wilson wants to know when I plan to return to duty."

"Do you have an answer for him?"

Frank shrugged. "I'm ready now, if he can use me."

"My guess, he'd tell you to stay here in the area until the relief effort is behind us. You've done a lot already."

Frank shook his head. "This is basic military operations."

"I hear you, but even the bishop mentioned your name this morning."

"He's a good man."

"So are you, Frank."

As much as he appreciated Colby's comment, Frank wasn't sure where he stood with the chief. Wilson was a competent investigator, but tight-lipped, especially with subordinates, and always faint on praise.

"I called Atlanta PD and left a message for Ulster to call me when he reports to work."

"Has anyone talked to Vivian?"

"Negative. The docs have her in an induced coma. I alerted security at the hospital on post and asked the military police to station a man outside her room."

"In case Trey returns?"

"Exactly. If he tried to kill her once, he may try again."

Would he come after Colleen, as well?

Frank let out a stiff breath. "Did anyone look at the call log on Vivian's phone?"

"We're waiting for a warrant, but I ran the plates on the blue Honda this morning."

"Colleen's car?"

Colby shrugged. "A long shot but you never know."

"You think she's lying."

"Look, Frank, we both know things aren't always as they seem. Her story's confusing enough that it just might be true, but as I mentioned last night, facts need to be verified. I wanted to ensure the car was registered to Colleen Brennan. I should hear something shortly."

"Keep me posted."

"Will do."

The coffee tasted bitter. Frank poured the remainder on the ground as Colby drove away. He crushed the recycled cardboard in his hand and tossed it in a nearby trash receptacle.

Duke had lost the keen sense of smell that had made him a valuable military working dog in the IED explosion in Afghanistan. Evidently, Frank had lost his investigative edge and ability to see things clearly, as well.

He hadn't even thought to run the plates.

In spite of what he had told Colleen last night, he wanted to believe her. The tale she had told—as Colby mentioned—seemed a bit disjointed, yet if all the pieces had been sewed too neatly together, he might have been even more suspicious.

The old Frank went on gut feelings, and his gut was telling him that Colleen was not involved in any criminal activity. He shook his head, knowing all too well that a sound investigation was based on facts, not feelings.

He couldn't let any personal feelings for Colleen get in the way of uncovering the truth. She was pretty and seemed legit, but as Colby said, looks could be deceiving. He thought of Audrey, which only drove home the fact that he wasn't a good judge of women.

Was Colleen to be trusted?

He hoped so, but he couldn't be sure.

Not with a supposed drug dealer turned killer like Trey Howard on the loose.

"What's wrong?" Evelyn asked, returning to the kitchen, where Colleen had fled, the fruit bowl still in hand, after seeing Ron's gold SUV. "I thought you were going with us. The food's in the car. Ron's ready to drive us down the hill."

"To the triage area?"

Evelyn nodded. "By the Amish Craft Shoppe."

As Frank had mentioned and where Colleen needed to go to find her purse.

Ron entered the kitchen and looked expectantly at Evelyn. "Are you ready?"

"I was just checking to ensure we got everything." After grabbing two additional serving utensils, she nodded. "I'm ready."

Evelyn pointed to the door and motioned Colleen forward. "Let's get the fruit in the car, and we'll be able to leave. People are hungry. We should hurry."

Ron and Evelyn were both staring at Colleen. She had to make a decision. Was Ron in any way involved with Trey? Or was it pure coincidence that the seemingly compassionate churchgoer had transported an injured man, who turned out to be a drug trafficker determined to cause her harm?

Colleen wasn't sure about Ron, but she trusted Evelyn, and she had to get back to her car. She'd go with them, but she'd keep her eyes open and watch for any signs that he wasn't who he seemed. For Evelyn's sake, she hoped Ron was a good man. For her own sake, as well.

SEVEN

Frank recognized Ron's gold SUV heading down the hill from Evelyn's house. The retired teacher was a nice guy who had been hanging around his sister recently.

Evelyn had been in love once, but she never talked about the guy or what had happened to break them up. Frank had been stationed at Fort Lewis, in Washington State.

About that same time, Evelyn had been involved in a car accident on a wet, slippery road that left her with a noticeable limp. Frank came home to help her recuperate. When he broached the subject about the former boyfriend, she had shrugged off his questions and indicated she didn't want to revisit the past. Frank had abided by her wishes. Now she seemed enamored with Ron, which made Frank happy for her sake.

Ron pulled onto the gravel path and braked to a stop. He waved as he stepped from his vehicle. "Hey there, Frank. We brought breakfast. Where do you want us?"

Frank looked past Evelyn and saw Colleen in the backseat. Her face appeared even more strained than when he'd seen her earlier in Evelyn's kitchen. They'd parted last night on an angry note, and he wanted to reassure her.

Colleen had nothing to worry about if she was telling the truth, but that was what hung heavy between them.

The uncertainty of whether she was being truthful about her involvement in Trey Howard's drug operation.

Frustrated that everything seemed so complicated, even in the light of day, he turned back to Ron and pointed him toward the clearing. "You can set up your serving line in front of the tent."

The teacher helped Evelyn from the car. Frank hurried to assist Colleen, but she opened her door before he could reach for the handle.

She stepped from the backseat, looking almost hesitant, and glanced at the barn, where one wall still hung precariously over her car.

Ron pulled out the first of four folding tables from the back of the SUV. Frank helped with the setup. Once the tables were upright, Evelyn wiped them with a damp cloth, and Colleen dried them with paper towels.

"You were up early this morning," Frank told his sister.

"I was saying my morning prayers and giving thanks to the Lord for saving us in the storm. Knowing people needed food, I wanted to get a head start on the breakfast casseroles. As it was, Ron arrived soon after you left and just as I was ready to pull them from the oven."

"Perfect timing." Frank's gaze flicked to Colleen, who had yet to say anything. Her cheeks had more color, but lines of fatigue were noticeable around her eyes.

She wore an emerald-green sweater, and her hair was pulled into a bun at the base of her neck. He followed her to the SUV and took a large bowl of fresh fruit from her hands.

"How's that lump on your forehead?" he asked.

"It's fine, but I'm worried about Vivian. Do you have any news about her condition?"

"The hospital wouldn't tell me much when I called

this morning. Only that she's still in ICU, and her condition's critical."

"Has anyone talked to her husband?"

Frank shook his head. "I'm not sure. CID may have."

"He didn't know about the trip to Colombia."

"That will have to be determined."

Colleen bristled.

"It's the way law enforcement operates, Colleen. Anecdotal information needs to be checked. We can't operate on hearsay."

Her eyes were guarded as she glanced up at him. "You think I'm covering up the truth?"

"I didn't say that."

"You didn't have to. You keep demanding answers to your questions, then when I provide information, you instantly discount it as not being factual."

She slipped on insulated mitts and grabbed one of the piping-hot casseroles. "I'd be better off not telling you anything, Frank. Then you could learn everything on your own, which you seem to need to do no matter what I say."

She huffed as she walked past him.

Anyone else and he wouldn't have been affected, but Colleen's sharp reproach made him flinch internally. She was right about his need to verify everything she said, but that was what investigators did, even when they believed a witness was being truthful.

He glanced at his sister, who didn't have a clue about what was going on. Ron was equally in the dark. Both of them smiled and chatted amicably as they transported the food from the SUV to the tables.

Two more carloads of volunteers parked near the Amish Craft Shoppe. They hustled forward carrying casseroles that, coupled with what Ron and Evelyn had brought, would provide an abundance of food for the workers and those displaced.

The military planned to set up a second tent this afternoon that would serve as a makeshift chow hall. Hot food in marmite containers was scheduled to arrive later in the day.

Ron would probably still be here helping out any way he could. Evelyn couldn't stand that long and would need a break. Colleen had to be tired, too.

Frank hadn't slept much last night, and he doubted she had either. He'd encourage her to rest, although he doubted she would want his advice.

A line of hungry rescue workers formed even before all the food had been placed on the tables. Ron raised his hands to get everyone's attention and offered a blessing over the food.

Colleen clasped her hands and lowered her eyes. A breeze played with a strand of hair that had come free from her neck. She pulled it behind her ear, her gaze still downward.

As Ron concluded the prayer, three flatbed trucks hauling bulldozers and backhoes came into view. American Construction was stenciled on the side of the earthmoving machinery.

Frank double-timed to the edge of the road and signaled where the vehicles should park. A man climbed down from the first truck. He wore a gray T-shirt with the construction company's logo of a bulldozer superimposed over a stenciled outline of the world.

Frank stretched out his hand and introduced himself. "You're the owner of American Construction?"

The big guy nodded. "Steve Nelson. I saw the report on the Atlanta news and called city hall in Freemont. They connected me to the mayor who's running the rescue effort. I told him we had some equipment and wanted to help."

The guy was built, at least six-two with huge biceps and a lot of definition under his shirt.

Steve wasn't a stranger to the gym. His strong grip and powerful forearm were evident when he shook Frank's hand.

"We appreciate the help."

The guy looked as Frank had at one time when weight lifting and training had been part of his daily routine.

"Frank Gallagher, Army CID. Nice to have you join us, Steve."

Two of his men approached, both big guys wearing the same company T-shirt and packing plenty of muscle. "Paul Yates and Kyle Ingram."

They shook hands. "Thanks so much," Frank said.

He filled them in on the stretch of homes that needed to be cleared along the road.

"There's food, if you want to grab some chow before you get started."

Steve held up his hand. "We ate before we left Atlanta."

Assessing the situation quickly, he sent one of the trucks farther south to connect with the effort closer to post.

"Paul and I'll get started here." Steve eyed the homes across the road still buried in debris. "You've completed the search for injured?"

"We have. Any structure that has a large X on its door has been cleared and is ready for your men."

He nodded. "We've done this a number of times over the twelve years our company's been in operation. Just tell me where you want me to start."

Frank pointed to the Craft Shoppe. Damage to the

building was minimal, but fallen trees and debris littered the entranceway. "Having the Amish store open for business would lift everyone's spirits."

Steve nodded. "We'll start there. Then head across the street and work south."

"Sounds like a plan."

Frank hustled back to the breakfast line. Colleen stood next to Evelyn, and both of them offered smiles of encouragement along with the food they dished up to the hungry workers.

Colleen chatted amicably with one of the men in line. More of her hair had pulled from the bun and blew free. For an instant, Frank had a vision of who Colleen really was. She seemed relaxed and embraced life. An inner beauty that she tried to mask was evident in the attention she showered on each person in line.

In that same moment, Frank wished he could be one of the people with whom she was interacting. Each time he and Colleen were together, she closed down, as if burdened by the weight she carried. He wanted to see her smile and hear her laughter.

Duke nuzzled close to Frank's leg as if sensing his master's confusion about the woman from Atlanta. Colleen may have told him the truth last night, but she was still embroiled in a shooting. The video found in her car only compounded the situation.

Frank needed to tread carefully. She could be hiding something behind her guarded gaze and cautious nature. He couldn't make a mistake and allow an attractive woman to throw him off course. He may be physically compromised, but he needed to think clearly.

She was someone of interest. The problem was, a part of him was interested in a way that didn't mesh with his

CID background. He needed to hold his feelings in check and use his brain instead of his heart when he was dealing with Colleen.

"Do you need anything?"

Colleen startled at the sound of Frank's voice. She turned to find him behind her, standing much too close. Needing space, she took a step back, but her leg hit the table.

Wanting to maintain her self-control, she raised her chin and stared up at his angular face. For one long moment, the hustle and bustle around her melted into the background. Her breath caught in her throat, and she forgot about his questions and the doubt she had heard in his voice the night before.

Just that quickly, reason returned. "I have everything I need, but thanks for checking."

Seemingly satisfied by her response, he moved on to Evelyn and asked her the same question.

Colleen turned back to the hungry people in line. Serving food to the workers lifted her spirits. She was grateful for the continuing assortment of breakfast casseroles, baked goods and fresh fruit that poured in from people in Freemont who wanted to help. The long line of hungry rescue personnel included firefighters and emergency personnel as well as military from Fort Rickman who appreciated the home-cooked meal.

The clip-clop of horses' hooves signaled the approach of Amish families in their buggies. Frank greeted the men with a handshake and offered words of welcome to the women and children. Duke frolicked with the youngsters, and they giggled as he licked their hands and wagged his tail.

As the families approached, the workers backed up to let those who had lost much move to the front of the line.

One of the men—evidently a spokesman for the Amish group—held up his hand. "We will wait our turn. We do not want to inconvenience you who are so willing to help us in our need."

"Please," a rescue worker insisted, speaking for the others in line. "You and your family need to eat. You've lost much."

"God provides," the man said with a nod. "We appreciate your generosity."

He motioned his family forward. Others followed. The eager faces of the children, when they held out their plates, hinted at their hunger.

Colleen was impressed by the children's politeness and the way they deferred to their parents. The mothers remained close and pointed to the various foods each child could take.

One little boy with blond hair and blue eyes took two bananas and then glanced at his mother, who shook her head ever so slightly.

The child quickly returned the extra piece of fruit and looked up at Colleen. "I must only take what I can eat and leave the rest for others."

He couldn't have been more than six or seven, but his demeanor and the apology he offered were that of a much older child.

During a lull in the line, she felt something rub against her leg and looked down to find Duke at her feet. She laughed at the sweet dog and watched him scamper off when Frank called his name.

He bent to pat the dog's neck, then glancing up, he stared at Colleen. Her heart skittered in her chest, and longing for some normalcy in her life swelled within her. If only she had met Frank under different circumstances.

A man in uniform tapped his shoulder, and Frank turned away. Suddenly, she felt alone in the midst of so many.

"I'm looking for a job to fill," a middle-aged woman said some minutes later as she approached Colleen. "Ron told me you need a break."

Although she was capable of working longer, Colleen knew the woman was eager to get involved.

"A break sounds good."

She looked for Frank and saw him in the distance. He was working with other military men setting up tables and chairs where people could sit while eating their meals. A large generator was humming, and fifty-cup coffeepots had been plugged into the electrical outlets. The smell of fresh-perked coffee wafted past her in the gentle breeze, and many people were enjoying the hot brew.

A ramp extended from the end of a flatbed truck. A man in a gray T-shirt drove a bulldozer down the incline and off the truck.

With a grateful nod, Colleen handed her serving utensil to the newcomer. The woman instantly began chatting with the people in line.

Retreating to the side of the military tent, Colleen grabbed a bottle of water from an ice chest. The cold liquid tasted good and refreshed her.

Everyone was busy, and no one seemed to miss her. After downing the last of the water, she dropped the bottle in one of the temporary trash receptacles and wiped her hands on her jeans. She glanced at the barn, where the back end of her car was visible under the wreckage.

Rubbing her forehead, Colleen mentally retraced her

movements yesterday. Usually she kept her purse in the passenger seat, but as she pulled into the rest stop, she'd tossed it into the rear to make room for Vivian.

Again, she checked to ensure no one needed her. Evelyn was chatting with one of the Amish ladies. The other servers seemed content doing their jobs and were focused on feeding the workers and Amish who continued to arrive by buggy.

Seeing that Frank was still tied up with the military, she hurried to the barn area, gingerly picked her way through the downed timber and ducked under the crime scene tape. She peered through the back window into her car but saw nothing except broken glass.

Rounding to the passenger side, she leaned over the front seat, shoved her fingers between the rear seat cushions and sighed with frustration when she came up empty-handed.

In the distance, the bulldozer gathered downed tree branches. The driver piled them to the edge of the road, where they could easily be picked up and carted off later in the day.

Colleen rounded the Honda, only this time, she grabbed the beams that blocked the driver's door and shoved them aside. The wood was heavy, and her energy was quickly sapped, but she continued to work, intent on having access into the rear of her car, behind the driver's seat. Without doubt, she'd wake up sore tomorrow, but finding her purse would be worth the effort.

Her neck was damp, and her hands ached, but she smiled with success when she cleared away the last of the rubble. Opening the driver's door, she saw what she was looking for—a small leather handbag wedged under the driver's seat. The clasp had come open, and the purse was empty.

She stretched her hand under the seat and patted the floorboard, searching for the spilled contents. She found a lipstick and a comb and placed both items in her bag. Once again, she used her hand to search along the floorboard.

Please, Lord.

A sense of relief spread over her when her fingers curled around her wallet. Pulling it free, she ensured her credit cards, driver's license and airline identification were still inside.

The roar of the bulldozer grew louder.

She glanced at the food line, which had started to thin. Time was of the essence. Ron and Evelyn would begin cleaning the area once all the people had been fed.

But she still needed the memory card.

An Amish teen appeared from the rear of the barn. He stared at her for a long moment and then walked quickly to where the others were eating.

A nervous flutter rumbled through her stomach at the young man and the pensive look he had given her.

Someone screamed. Colleen turned at the sound and saw Evelyn staring at the barn with her hands over her mouth. Ron was standing next to the young Amish boy. In the distance, she saw Frank running toward her, as if in slow motion.

For the briefest second, Colleen wondered what had caused them concern. Then she heard the *whoosh* of air and the *creak* and *groan* of wood. Glancing up, she saw the lone portion of wall still standing. Only now it was crashing down around her.

She ducked and raised her hands to protect her head. The purse dropped to her feet, its contents spilling onto the ground.

The last thing she heard was Frank's voice. He was screaming her name.

EIGHT

Heart in his throat, Frank followed the ambulance to the Freemont hospital. He'd been the first to get to Colleen. Medical personnel were close by to respond to the emergency. They'd started an IV line, taken her vitals and then hastened to get her into the ambulance that was currently racing along River Road to Freemont.

Frank's phone rang. Relieved the cell tower was back in operation, he glanced at Colby's name on the monitor and pushed Talk. "What'd you find out?"

"The guy driving the bulldozer was Paul Yates. He claimed he'd checked the barn and hadn't seen anyone in the area before he picked up the first load of fallen timbers. According to him, he didn't get near the wall. Steve Nelson, the construction team boss, told me Paul was a conscientious worker and doubted that his man, even inadvertently, would have knocked the load he was carrying against the edge of the barn wall."

Frank sighed, frustrated at his own mistake. "If he did cause the wall to topple, I have to take some of the blame. I told Steve his men could clear the area around the Craft Shoppe. The store's structure was in good shape. I thought the sooner we start getting some of the businesses and homes restored, the better."

"Which was sound reasoning. You're not at fault,

Frank. Yates probably thought he'd clean up around the barn, although—as I mentioned—he said he never saw anyone in the area."

"Colleen was standing in plain sight by the car."

"That's what Ron Malone told me. He verified she was clearly visible when the wall came down, but she could have been hunkered down and peering into her car when Paul checked. If he checked."

Frank glanced at the purse he'd pulled from under the fallen timber, which she must have found. Colleen had wanted to retrieve her identification and credit cards, yet nothing was worth putting her life in danger.

"Your sister said to let her know when you hear from the doctor," Colby added.

"Will do. Make sure Ron takes her home so she can rest. She not only looked upset but also exhausted. She worked late last night and was back at it this morning."

"They plan to leave soon."

"Have you heard anything from Atlanta PD?"

"Negative."

"What about the check on the Honda's plates?"

"I'm not sure what the holdup is. I'll give them another call."

"Let me know."

"Will do."

"Thanks, Colby." Frank hesitated for a long moment, choosing his words. "For being there, for helping."

"You mean calming you down? It wasn't your fault she was injured."

"She's staying at my sister's house. I feel responsible. I should have posted a guard at the barn."

"That's not CID's jurisdiction. The Freemont police needed to get involved, although everyone's overworked at this point. I don't know if you heard the news. The governor called in the National Guard, but he sent them farther east to Macon, where a second tornado touched down. According to the radio report I heard, he's satisfied Freemont is well taken care of with Fort Rickman's help."

"Only Rickman has their own damage to repair." The hospital appeared in the distance. "We're approaching the medical facility. I'll call you once the doctor makes his diagnosis."

Frank kept his focus on the ambulance ahead of him. The siren wailed as the EMT at the wheel entered the intersection leading to the medical complex. Frank followed close behind.

He kept seeing the wall crash down on Colleen. He hadn't been able to get there fast enough and had frantically clawed at the fallen timbers to save her. He'd found her dazed and bleeding from a head wound that was all too close to the blow she'd taken yesterday, which made him even more concerned.

The EMTs had been concerned, as well. They'd used a backboard and neck brace to stabilize her spine and had hurried her into an ambulance.

He hoped she wouldn't have any permanent injury or hadn't suffered internal wounds that would need further medical care.

The ambulance braked to a stop in front of the ER. The automatic doors opened, and medical personnel wearing pale green scrubs raced to meet their patient.

The EMTs lowered the gurney to the pavement and pushed her into the hospital. Nurses hovered close by, assessing her injuries as they rushed Colleen into a trauma room.

Frank found a nearby parking space and hurried inside. A nurse pointed him to a room where even more medical staff surrounded the gurney where she lay.

"Can you hear me?" a doctor questioned.

A nurse grabbed the telephone. "We've got an injury in trauma room two. I need a CBC and chemistry panel. Protime and PTT. Type and cross for two units." She nodded. "I'll place the order now."

After returning the phone to its cradle, she typed the lab orders on a nearby computer.

"BP's 130 over 70," a voice called out. "Pulse 65."

The doctor checked her pupils and had Colleen follow his finger with her eyes. All the while her head was immobilized on the backboard.

He glanced at Frank, hovering near the doorway. "Family?"

"Ah, no. I'm with the CID."

"Is she a victim of a crime?"

"Negative. Her injury was accidental."

"Then I need you to leave the room and give the patient privacy."

Frank understood the doctor's request, but he didn't want to leave Colleen. He knew how fast things could go south if an internal injury was involved.

When the medics had taken him to the field hospital in Afghanistan, he'd been in good shape. Or so everyone had thought. Too quickly his blood pressure had bottomed out. He'd gone into shock and had been rushed into surgery—the first of many.

As Colleen was being lifted into the ambulance, Evelyn had grabbed his hand. The concern in her eyes had made him aware of how much she understood the emotions that were playing havoc with his control.

"I'm praying for Colleen," she'd assured him.

Knowing his sister's deep faith and her belief in prayer had brought a bit of calm in the midst of his turmoil. Evelyn would storm heaven, of that Frank could be sure.

He wanted to stand in the hallway outside the trauma room, but a nurse escorted him to a waiting area. She promised to notify him if there was any change in Colleen's condition. Not that he could sit idly by. He paced from the door to the bay of windows on the far wall and back again, feeling trapped and confined, like a caged animal.

He looked down, expecting to find Duke at his feet and needing his calm support, but Evelyn had kept the dog with her.

Every time the door opened, Frank hoped to see one of Colleen's nurses.

No one appeared whom he recognized. He glanced at his watch. The ambulance had arrived more than thirty minutes ago. How long would the medical team take before he would receive word of her injuries?

He pulled out his phone and checked his emails, searching especially for a message from Special Agent in Charge Wilson. Frank was ready to get back on active duty. Surely Wilson could use him.

Of course, the chief might not be willing to take a chance on him. Especially after the witness Frank needed to keep safe had been injured.

The door opened, and the nurse from Colleen's room motioned him forward.

"An aide is transporting Colleen Brennan to X-ray. They should return in a few minutes. The doctor will review the X-rays and test results once they're back from the lab. If you want to wait in her room, you can."

Relieved, Frank headed for the trauma room. His stomach tightened when he saw droplets of blood on the floor.

His mind went wild with concern. "You mentioned X-rays. Does that mean internal injuries?"

"The X-rays will tell us a lot. The doctor may order a CT scan."

Bile rose in Frank's throat. He glanced at the vinyl chair shoved in the corner and knew he couldn't sit. Backtracking to the doorway, he peered into the hall, hoping to catch sight of Colleen.

Where was she? What was her condition? What was the doctor keeping from him?

The sound of a gurney rolling over the tile floor flooded him with relief. She was alert, and her color was good. The backboard had been removed, which was another positive sign.

"Did you find the Amish boy?"

Frank didn't understand what she was saying.

"You saw him, didn't you?" she insisted. "He came out from behind the barn just before the wall toppled."

"What'd he look like?"

"Straw hat, blue shirt, suspenders."

The same as every other Amish kid. "You think he caused the wall to fall?"

"I don't know. Ask Ron. He talked to him."

"Will do, but what about you?"

"I'm okay." She grimaced. "Except for my head."

"Another concussion?"

"They haven't told me yet. The patient's the last to know."

He followed the gurney into the room. The nurse's aide held up her hand. "Give us a minute, sir, until I get Ms. Brennan settled."

"Oh, sure. Sorry." He returned to the hallway. The door closed behind him.

Colleen needed her privacy. Shame on him for barging into her room.

He started to call Colby about the Amish boy, then

disconnected when the door to Colleen's room opened. The aide scurried down the hall.

Frank waited a long moment, wondering if she would return.

He hesitated too long.

Another health-care worker, wearing a white lab coat, entered the trauma room and closed the door.

Frank shook his head with frustration. At this rate, he might never see Colleen. Patience had never been his strong suit, except when he pulled surveillance. Today's wait seemed especially trying.

The main thing was to ensure Colleen was okay.

His cell rang. Colby's number.

Frank raised the mobile device to his ear. "Did you find out anything?"

"Can you talk?"

Frank's gut tightened. Needing to speak freely, he headed for the empty waiting room. Colby had information to share, but from the negative overtones in his voice, the news wasn't good.

Did it involve Colleen?

Colleen hadn't expected Frank to follow her to the hospital and then wait while the various tests were being run. She thought he had stayed behind. Spotting him in the hallway when she came back from X-ray had been a surprise that added a hint of brightness to a very bleak day.

Although from what she knew about Frank, he probably wanted to question her about breaking through the crime scene tape. Was it against the law to search for her own missing purse?

She closed her eyes and tried to relax. Knowing Frank was in the hallway made her doubly anxious.

The door opened, and someone—no doubt, Frank—

entered the room. Unwilling to face the confrontation she expected to see in his eyes, she pretended to be asleep.

His footsteps were heavy as he neared the gurney.

She sensed him staring down at her.

Unnerved, she opened her eyes.

She didn't see Frank.

She saw Trey.

NINE

Colleen screamed. Trey hovered over her. He raised his hand and pressed it across her nose and mouth, cutting off her air supply and blocking any additional sound she tried to make.

She writhed and scratched his face, then grabbed his nose and twisted.

He growled and clamped his hand down even harder.

Unable to breathe, she thrashed at him, kicked her feet and shifted her weight. The gurney was narrow, and the sheet covering the vinyl pad shifted with her.

With one massive thrust, she threw her legs up and over the narrow edge. Gravity helped.

She fell to the floor, along with the sheet.

Trey lost his hold.

Gasping for air, she crawled away from him like a crab.

He reached for her again.

She kicked and screamed.

Where was Frank?

Why wouldn't he come to her rescue?

"I got a call from Ulster," Colby said.

The cop in Atlanta. Frank shoved the cell closer to his ear.

"The two women Colleen mentioned who were murdered worked at the King's Club. Guess who else worked there up until four months ago?"

"You tell me."

"Briana Doyle."

"Colleen's sister."

"Roger that."

An interesting twist. "Anything else?"

"He also said Sutherland—that Atlanta cop who gave Colleen a hard time—suffered a nervous breakdown and had to retire."

"What about the plates on the Honda?"

"The car's registered to a Ms. C. A. Brennan."

Frank couldn't help but smile. "Do me a favor, Colby. See if anyone remembers an Amish teen hanging around the barn today."

"Do you have a name?"

"Negative, but Colleen saw him talking to Ron Malone."

"Evelyn's friend?"

A sound filtered into the waiting room, like a muffled cry.

Frank tensed. "Hold for a minute."

Lowering the phone, he retraced his steps into the hallway and listened.

A woman screamed.

Colleen!

Someone ran down the corridor.

Six foot. Stocky. White lab coat.

Frank's heart stopped. He crashed into her room. Colleen was on the floor, back to the wall.

She shook her head and pointed to the hall. "I'm not hurt. Go after him."

Frank raced into the corridor.

The man rounded the corner at the end of the hallway. Frank followed.

A nurse blocked his path.

He shoved past her.

A lab technician carrying a tray with tubes of blood appeared.

"Get back," Frank yelled. He sailed around her and turned left. The hall was empty.

Glancing back, he spotted a stairwell.

Frank shoved open the heavy fire door. A short stairway led to an emergency exit, leading out of the hospital.

He bounded down the steps.

Movement behind him.

Frank turned. A fire extinguisher sailed through the air, aimed straight for him. He lifted his hands to block the hit.

The canister crashed against his chest, knocked air from his lungs and forced him off balance. He fell down the steps. His head scraped against the wall.

The stairwell door opened, and the man in the lab coat walked back into the hospital.

Frank's ears rang. Pain screamed through his body. Fighting to remain conscious, he groped for his cell and heard Colby's voice.

"What's going on, Frank?"

He'd never disconnected.

"Someone attacked Colleen." Frank struggled to his feet. "A guy wearing a white lab coat. Six foot. Stocky. Call hospital security. Tell them to lock down the facility."

Frank grabbed the banister and pulled himself up the stairs. "Notify Freemont PD. The attack happened in trauma room two in the ER. He was last seen in the rear stairwell."

"Where'd he go from there?"

Back to Colleen!

Ice froze Frank's veins.

He jerked open the fire door and stumbled into the hallway.

"Colleen," he screamed, racing back to her.

Hurling himself into the trauma room, he expected the worst.

She sat crumpled on the floor, her face twisted with fear.

"Frank." She gasped with relief. Tears sprang from her eyes.

He was on his knees at her side, reaching for her. She collapsed into his arms. He pulled her trembling body close, feeling her warmth. Hot tears dampened his neck.

She was alive. Relief swept over him. A lump of gratitude filled his throat. He hadn't lost her. Not this time, but he hadn't reacted fast enough. She'd almost died because of his inability to protect her.

He rubbed his hand over her slender shoulders. "Shh. I've got you. You're safe."

For now. But someone wanted to kill her. Whether she had been working with Trey or against him, he was determined to end her life.

Trey would come back. No doubt about it. Would Frank be able to save her the next time?

TEN

"He must have headed down the east corridor and left from that side of the hospital," Frank had told the hospital security earlier and now repeated the details to the Freemont police officer who had answered the call.

The cop was pushing fifty with a full face and tired eyes. His name tag read Talbot. He had pulled a tablet and pen from his pocket and was making note of the information Frank provided.

As Talbot wrote, Frank rubbed his side that had taken the hit. The fire extinguisher had bruised a couple of ribs and the area around one of his incisions. The dull ache was aggravating but not serious.

Colleen was resting in the ER room across the hall, awaiting the doctor's decision about whether she would be released or admitted for observation. Frank had wanted to stay with her, but Talbot insisted on questioning Frank in private. The only way he would leave Colleen was if the door to her room and the door to the room across the hall where Frank now sat both remained opened.

The cop looked up from his notebook. "Did you see his face?"

"Only in profile, but Ms. Brennan gave you a description."

"That's correct. I just wanted verification."

Law enforcement's need to confirm anecdotal information was what Frank had tried to explain to Colleen. Now, as his own irritation began to mount, he understood her frustration.

"The man was approximately six feet tall, wearing a white lab coat. I can't be sure about his build. He appeared stocky. Muscular might be a better description."

"Ms. Brennan thought you were in the hallway. She screamed, but you failed to respond." The cop paused and pursed his lips. "Did she imagine raising her voice?"

"As I mentioned earlier, I went into the waiting room to take a call. Hearing a sound, I retraced my steps and realized Ms. Brennan was in distress."

"The person who phoned you was—"

Colby was busy dealing with the Amish. Frank didn't want him tied up, answering Talbot's questions, especially when Frank was at fault for letting Trey escape.

He scrubbed his hands over his face. What was wrong with him these days?

"The name?" the cop pressed.

"Special Agent Voss."

"First name?"

More irritation bubbled up within Frank. "Special Agent Colby Voss."

"Spelled?"

How else would Voss be spelled? "V.O.S.S." The cop was a jerk. Either that or he had a bone to pick with the military.

Needing to reassure himself that Colleen was all right, Frank glanced through the two open doorways to where she was resting in the room across the hall. Her eyes were closed and her hands folded at her waist.

He pulled his gaze back to Talbot. Dark circles rimmed his eyes.

Frank's temper subsided ever so slightly.

"Have you been involved with the search and rescue?"

The cop nodded. "When I'm not cleaning up my own property. My wife and I live on the west side of town. The twister tore the roof off our house. The wife was inside." He shook his head and looked as dejected as Frank had felt when he realized Trey had escaped. "We're living with our daughter and son-in-law. They don't have room for us."

"I'm sorry."

"It's not your fault. My wife blames God, but it's not His fault either."

Frank's opinion of the cop did a one-eighty. Although hard to admit, deep down Frank had blamed God after the IED explosion and Audrey's rejection. It was easier to claim the Lord was at fault instead of his own poor judgment.

The doctor entered Colleen's room.

"If there's anything else you need from me, call my cell." Frank gave the cop his number as well as the one for Evelyn's landline.

"I'll alert local law enforcement to be on the lookout for Trey Howard. As you're probably aware, the department's working long shifts trying to keep the peace in the areas hardest hit by the storm. Doubt we'll be back to normal operations for a few more days, so I wouldn't hold your breath about tracking him down anytime soon."

The doctor stepped into the hallway and motioned to the nurse. "Once pharmacy fills the pain prescription for Ms. Brennan, she's free to go."

The nurse nodded. "I'll get her meds and discharge papers."

Frank climbed from the table and shook hands with

the cop. "I appreciate your help today. Let me know if you find out anything about Trey Howard."

"I've got your phone number, sir. I'll contact you first thing."

Frank left the room with a better attitude. He hated that he hadn't nabbed Trey, but he'd changed his opinion of the cop. The guy was carrying a lot on his shoulders.

He knocked on Colleen's open door. His heart softened when she looked up and smiled. She was carrying a lot, too. Her sister had died because of a drug dealer who seemed to escape apprehension. Frank had to find Trey before he hurt Colleen again.

Frank's head was scraped and he looked tired, but Colleen smiled when he stepped into her room. "Did you finish answering Talbot's questions?"

"The guy's thorough."

"Don't all of you law enforcement types follow the same playbook?"

He laughed. She liked the sound.

"How's the head?" he asked.

She shrugged. "Pain is relative. I'll survive."

"And the shoulder?"

"You mean where I hit the floor after I slipped off the gurney?"

Frank nodded.

"It's probably not as painful as that scrape on your forehead."

"You need to rest."

"That's what the doctor told me. Rest and protect my head. Two cranial blows in a short span of time aren't recommended for good health. The doc doesn't want me to end up like some old prizefighter. Research claims concussions don't lead to good quality of life."

"It's not something to joke about."

"I know, but if I don't laugh, I just might cry. That wouldn't be good."

"Sometimes shedding a few tears helps."

The nurse returned to the room and dropped a plastic medicine bottle in Colleen's hand. "Take every six hours as needed for pain. They'll make you sleepy. Don't operate motor vehicles when taking them."

"My car was totaled in the storm," Colleen said.

"Tough break, huh?" The nurse sorted through the papers she carried. "Have someone check on you in the night."

She handed Colleen the release instructions. "This covers most of the questions you might have. The doctor warned you to guard your head, and don't take any more hits."

Colleen smiled. "He mentioned that might be a problem."

"He's right. Be extra careful."

"I don't plan to get into any more dangerous situations."

"Could I get that in writing?" Frank asked.

The nurse pointed to the scrape on his forehead as she left the room. "As if you should talk."

Colleen turned to Frank when they were alone. "Thank you for going after Trey. I wouldn't be here if it weren't for you." She held out her hand and gripped his in a half shake, half high-five motion.

"I didn't react fast enough," he countered.

The nurse knocked and pushed the wheelchair through the door.

"I'll drive the car to the front of the hospital." Frank hurried to the parking lot.

"He seems like a nice guy." The nurse helped Colleen off the gurney and into the wheelchair.

"He's not sure what he wants in life."

"I can relate. I still don't know what I want to do when I grow up."

Colleen raised her brow. "But you've got a great profession."

"Sometimes I want more in life. Money, fame."

"Really? I just want to be safe."

The nurse patted her hand. "Looks like you've got a special guy who's all about protection."

Colleen was taken aback. Surely she wasn't talking about Frank?

"His face softens when he looks at you," the nurse added. "I'd say he's interested."

Colleen shrugged off the statements about Frank because they weren't true. The nurse was wrong, although Colleen would like having someone to protect her. Especially if that someone was Frank Gallagher.

ELEVEN

Frank called Evelyn and filled her in on what had happened after he and Colleen left the hospital. She was understandably upset about the attack and concerned about Colleen's well-being.

"Is Ron there?" he asked.

"He left a short while ago, why?"

"Just wondering." He didn't mention the Amish boy Colleen had seen earlier. Evelyn didn't need anything more to add to her concern.

"Be careful," she warned before they disconnected.

Lowering his cell, he glanced at Colleen. "Evelyn's worried about you."

"And I'm worried about putting both of you in danger."

"Hey, remember—" he pointed a finger back at himself "—I'm with law enforcement and used to dealing with criminals."

"Yes, but Evelyn doesn't need to get involved."

"She's not in danger, and with the BOLO out on Trey, he'll be in custody before long."

Colleen tugged at a strand of her hair. "I'm not as optimistic as you are. Trey's cunning. He tells a lonely woman lies she wants to hear and gets her to smuggle drugs into this country. If she balks, he overdoses her or shoots her at a roadside park. He doesn't think of anyone but himself."

She glanced out the window and sighed. "Maybe I should hole up in a motel someplace. You don't need trouble underfoot."

"And prevent Evelyn from extending her gracious Southern hospitality?"

"I don't want anyone else to get hurt."

He reached for her hand. "You're not going to a motel. Evelyn wouldn't think of it, and neither would I. Plus—" he smiled "—Duke's a good watchdog."

She smiled back, and relief swept over him. He squeezed her hand to reassure her and almost groaned when his cell rang. The last thing he wanted was to pull his hand away from hers.

He glanced at the screen and hit Talk. "Yeah, Colby."

"I tried to contact Ron Malone, but I couldn't reach him. Seems there were a number of teenage Amish boys getting a free breakfast this morning. I need a name or something to distinguish the kid in question from every other Amish youth."

"Ron was at my sister's house for most of the afternoon. Colleen and I are headed there now. I'll call him." Frank paused, wondering if Colby had anything additional to add.

"Stay safe," was all he said before disconnecting.

Seems everyone was worried about their well-being.

Frank punched in Ron's home number.

"Good evening. Ron Malone speaking."

The guy was definitely old-school. "Ron, this is Frank Gallagher."

"How's Colleen? Evelyn phoned and filled me in."

"She's okay. I'm calling about the accident at the barn today. Do you remember talking to an Amish boy just before it collapsed? He's probably sixteen or seventeen years old. Straw hat. Suspenders."

"That would be Isaac Fisher. He and his sister, Martha, work at the Amish Craft Shoppe."

Frank glanced at Colleen and gave her a reassuring nod as Ron continued.

"Isaac's math skills need help so I've been tutoring him. We were trying to schedule our next session around the relief effort. Why do you ask?"

"He was hanging around the barn today."

"And probably had his eye on the Craft Shoppe. He wants to go back to work. Money's tight for most of the Amish, especially for a young guy who's planning for his future."

"Any reason to think he might have done something to cause the wall to topple?"

"You're saying it wasn't an accident?"

"I'm just asking for your opinion, Ron."

"Isaac Fisher is a fine young man who would never bring dishonor to himself or his family."

"That's what I wanted to hear. Thanks."

Lowering his cell, he smiled at Colleen. "Ron vouched for the teen. Isaac Fisher. Ron called him a fine young man."

"But—"

"You don't believe Ron?"

"I'm not sure." She wrapped her arms around her waist and stared out the window.

Frank watched her out of the corner of his eye. "Take one of those pain pills when we get to Evelyn's."

"I'm fine."

But, of course, she wasn't. Frank still had a lot of questions about the photo she'd sent to the Atlanta police, about her sister knowing the two women who had been killed and about why she was suspicious of an Amish boy who sounded like a good kid.

As fragile as Colleen seemed, this wasn't the time to delve into anything that would increase her anxiety. The doctor had ordered her to rest, which was what she needed.

Frank's questions could wait until morning. Everything would seem more clear then. At least, that was his hope.

Colleen couldn't pull her thoughts together. She kept feeling Trey's hand covering her mouth and nose. Shaking her head ever so slightly, she tried to scatter the memory and focus instead on being with Frank.

"Are you sure you're okay?" he asked, concern so evident in his voice.

"I'm trying *not* to think about what happened."

He nodded as if he understood, but how could he know what she was thinking? So many questions swirled through her mind. About the man in Atlanta who had been snooping around her apartment, about whether Ron Malone could be trusted and whether a young Amish boy could somehow be involved in Trey's drug operation.

She fingered her handbag, grateful that Frank had pulled it from the debris today. At least she had her identification, but what about the memory card?

Would she ever feel confident enough to tell Frank?

He didn't need to see the photo of her with men who worked for Trey. She'd been foolish to allow Trey to take the picture. Too late, she'd realized that he wanted the picture to blackmail her, in case she decided to go to the police.

She'd outsmarted Trey, but not for long. Now he was after her. No matter what Frank thought, Trey was dangerous, and he wouldn't stop until he found her. Knowing he had been with Ron after the storm troubled her even more.

Pulling in a deep breath, she had to tell Frank. "There's something I haven't mentioned."

He raised his brow but kept his gaze on the road.

"That first night, when the tornado touched down and then you found me—"

Frank nodded.

"I saw Trey with Ron Malone."

"Evelyn's Ron?"

"He drove Trey to the triage area."

"Ron transported a lot of folks that night." Frank glanced at her. "You took a bad hit to your head, Colleen. You couldn't remember a number of things. Are you sure you saw Trey?"

"I thought I did."

"You were frightened. Sometimes our minds play tricks on us."

"Maybe." Or maybe not. Colleen needed to find out the truth about Ron Malone and his relationship with Trey. Even if it put her in danger.

Colleen was quiet for the rest of the ride home. Frank helped her from the car, but she insisted on walking on her own.

Audrey had always sought his help and made him feel as if he was in charge. Looking back, she'd played him and fed his ego. Had he really been in love with her?

"Oh, Colleen, we were so worried." Evelyn gave her a warm hug when they got inside. She pointed to the scrape on Frank's forehead. "Looks like you and the doc came to fisticuffs."

Colleen tried to smile, then grimaced.

"You've got two choices." Frank ushered her into the kitchen and pulled out a chair at the table. "Sit down or head straight to bed."

"I'm fine."

Colleen had grit and determination, almost to a fault. She needed to let down that strong wall of independence at times. Like now, when she was shaky and her strength compromised.

The nurse had given them instructions. Colleen needed to be checked in the night. Nausea or a severe headache could signal life-threatening complications. She'd had one brush with death already. She didn't need any more problems tonight.

Frank pointed to the chair.

"If you insist." She sat, and he pushed her closer to the table.

"Can I fix you something to eat?" Evelyn asked.

"Is there any soup left?" Colleen asked.

"Of course." She glanced at Frank. "How about you? I doubt you've eaten today."

"Soup sounds good." Once his sister thought he needed nourishment, she wouldn't let up until he agreed to eat. He'd learned that early on after he moved in following his infection.

Of course, at that point, the MRSA had taken a toll on his body and nearly done him in. The highly contagious deadly organism he'd picked up in the hospital had been hard to overcome.

"Anything I can do to help?" he asked.

"Grab a couple placemats and some silverware. You know where the napkins are."

"You're not joining us?"

"I've already eaten." Evelyn glanced at the clock. "Ron's coming over. There's a new sitcom on television.

We were planning to watch it together, although I can tell him tonight might not be a good idea."

Colleen held up her hand. "Don't change your plans on account of me. I don't need to eat."

"Nonsense. I'll heat the soup and let Frank take over while I freshen up."

"Ron's visiting quite often these days." Frank set the table and winked at Colleen.

Fatigue rimmed her eyes and her face was even more pale than usual.

The doorbell rang.

"He's early." Evelyn's voice held a note of flustered alarm.

"Go. Put on your lipstick." Frank pointed to her bedroom. "I'll take care of the door and the soup." He smiled as his sister scurried from the kitchen.

Frank lowered the heat under the pan and then hurried to open the door.

"Good to see you," Ron said as soon as he stepped inside. He glanced into the kitchen, where Colleen sat. "We were all concerned about you today."

"I'm fine. Just a bit worn-out."

"Evelyn and I prayed for you." He pointed his thumb at Frank. "We've been praying for this guy for a long time."

"No wonder I'm doing so well." Frank smiled. "Colleen's tired but pretending to be stronger than she looks."

"That last part sounds like Evelyn."

"She'll join you in a minute, Ron. Can I get you some coffee or a cola?"

"Thanks, but I'll make myself at home in the den."

"I need to ask you something, Ron." Colleen sat up straighter in the chair. She glanced at Frank and then back at the former teacher. "The night of the storm, do you remember transporting a man in a black hooded sweatshirt to the triage area?"

"Sure do. He was the first of many who needed help. I found him walking along Amish Road. He was shook up and didn't have much to say except that the twister had picked up his car. No telling where it landed. I left him with the EMTs, who said they'd take care of him. Do you know the guy?"

Frank nodded. "We think he's the man who came after Colleen today."

Ron gasped. "I had no idea. Is he from around here?"

"Atlanta."

"What brought him to Freemont?"

"It's a long story."

Evelyn's footsteps sounded in the hallway. Ron turned his full attention to her when she entered the kitchen. Her cheeks glowed pink, and her eyes were bright and focused on Ron.

"The show's almost ready to start," she said, motioning him into the den.

"Enjoy the program." Frank turned back to the stove. Steam was rising from the pan. He stirred the soup and dished up two bowls, placing them on the table.

Settling into the chair across from Colleen, he smiled. "Are you okay with Ron?"

"I'm sorry about all the questions I asked."

"Evelyn's a good judge of character."

"She met him at church?"

"That's right. He's started to come over more often since I moved in." Frank hesitated. "I don't think he's involved with Trey."

"I'm sure you're right. It's nice that he's been praying for you."

Frank nodded. "I knew Evie prayed, but I didn't think other folks in her church were praying for me, as well."

"It may sound like a strange question, but how's that make you feel?" Colleen's gaze was intense.

"Humbled. At one point, the docs weren't sure I'd pull through. My sister must have spread the word that I needed prayer."

"Your injury was severe."

He nodded. "I walked into a building before Duke cleared it of explosives. Broke my pelvis and a few other bones."

Frank smiled down at the trusty dog at his feet. "Duke was scraped up pretty badly, but he stayed with me and alerted the guys who came looking for me the next day. I went to Lanstuhl in Germany for my first operation. Then Walter Reed. My final surgery was at Augusta, about five hours from here."

"Then you came here to recover?"

"Eventually. Somewhere along the line I was exposed to MRSA. My immune system was compromised, and I had a hard time fighting the infection."

He tried to smile. "You know how Evie likes to cook, which worked to my advantage since I'd lost so much weight and strength."

"Your sister's generous with her love." Colleen peered at Duke under the table. "How'd you end up with your sweet pup?"

As if knowing Colleen was talking about him, Duke pranced to her side of the table and sat at her feet.

"The explosion did something to his nose," Frank continued. "When a military working dog can't track a scent, he's forced to retire. I heard he was at Fort Rickman and asked if I could adopt him."

He smiled, watching as Colleen rubbed Duke's neck. "We've been through a lot together."

"Duke's probably enjoying retirement, but it sounds like you're ready to go back to work."

"That's my hope." Or was it?

Not wanting to open that door tonight, he pointed to the bowls of soup. "Dinner's getting cold."

"You're right." Colleen lowered her head.

"If you want to pray out loud, I'll join you."

She glanced up at him, seemingly startled.

"We both have a lot for which to be thankful."

Her face softened, and she smiled. Warmth spread through him.

Her hand was still on the table. He reached out and grasped it before his internal voice of reason could tell him to be cautious. After everything that had happened, he wanted to join Colleen in prayer, even if he didn't know what words to say. He'd let her lead this time. Maybe he'd be able to say his own prayers, in time.

After they finished the soup, Frank walked Colleen to the guest room and said good-night at the door.

"Is there anything you need?" he asked.

She shook her head, grateful for the concern she heard in his voice and the sincerity in his expression. Something had changed since the run-in with Trey at the hospital. Maybe Frank finally believed her.

"Thanks."

He raised his brow. "For saying good-night?"

She laughed. "For saving my life. If…if you hadn't been there—"

"I almost didn't make it in time."

"You scared Trey off."

"But he escaped."

"At that moment, all I cared about was staying alive."

The thought of what could have happened made her shiver.

Frank reached for her. She stepped closer, and his arms circled her shoulders. She laid her head on his shoulder.

Frank had to be as tired as she was, yet she could feel his strength and determination. He had saved her from Trey. She thought she could bring the drug dealer to justice on her own, but she needed help. She needed Frank.

At the moment, she didn't think of Frank as a cop. She thought of him as a man. He was tall and strong, even though he still wore some of the ravages of the infection he had battled.

Colleen had been so wrong about who he really was. Now she saw him in a better light, and she liked what she saw.

She allowed herself to rest in his embrace for a long moment before she pulled back. "Thanks again for today." She flipped on the overhead light in the bedroom. "If you'll excuse me, I'm tired and need to sleep."

Stepping into the room, she closed the door and sighed. Frank hadn't believed her last night. Did he now? She didn't know for sure.

Until she knew his true feelings, she had to be careful and guard her heart.

TWELVE

Colleen inhaled the clean smell of the outdoors as she snuggled between the crisp sheets—no doubt dried on the line—and pulled the quilt up to her shoulders. Feeling pampered by the fresh linens, she fell asleep quickly and woke with a start some hours later from a dream that seemed too real.

She saw Trey in the woods, rifle raised, and heard Vivian's cry for help, along with the deafening roar of the twister.

Throwing back the covers, Colleen grabbed the robe Evelyn had provided and shrugged into the soft cotton. Reaching to turn on the bedside lamp, she hesitated, her hand in midair.

A sound upset the stillness.

With every nerve on high alert, she turned her ear toward the double French doors leading to the porch and strained to decipher the sound that came again.

Metal on metal?

Ever so quietly, she slipped from the bed and tiptoed to the window. With her back to the wall, she lifted the edge of the curtain.

Darkness.

Staring into the black night, she willed her eyes to focus. Slowly, they adjusted.

Movement.

Snip. Then another.

Her pulse raced and fear clawed at her throat.

The sound repeated over and over again.

She strained to make out some faint outline that could identify who was trying to gain access.

There. A hand thrust through the porch screen.

A portion of the wire mesh pulled free.

She dropped the curtain and turned to flee.

Tired though he was, Frank couldn't sleep. He kept seeing Colleen buried in the rubble, first when the twister hit and then later when the barn wall had collapsed on top of her. He'd screamed and raced forward, but he couldn't get to Colleen in time.

Thankfully, the roof of the Honda had stopped the momentum of the wall's downward collapse. Colleen had been hit by broken boards, but not with the full force of the larger section.

He'd asked Evie to check on Colleen during the night. No doubt, his sister was also giving thanks to the Lord about the right resolution to a very dangerous situation today. Frank wasn't used to turning to God, yet a swell of gratitude rose within him.

Dropping his legs over the side of the bed, he sat up and stared into the darkness. "I don't know what to say except thank you, Lord."

Satisfied with his first significant attempt in years to communicate directly with the Almighty, Frank lay back down, hoping to grab some shut-eye.

Duke stirred at the foot of the bed.

"Easy, boy. What is it?"

The dog whined and trotted to the door.

"You hear something?"

He pranced and whined again.

Frank stood, slipped into a pair of jeans and grabbed his service weapon.

Opening the door ever so carefully, he glanced at the door to Evelyn's bedroom and stepped into the hallway. Duke trotted toward the kitchen and turned into the rear hallway leading to the sewing room, where Colleen now slept.

Frank followed and stopped outside Colleen's room. All he heard was the beat of his heart and the dog's even breaths at his feet.

Had he imagined something?

Duke had seemed a bit skittish since the tornado. Both of them were having problems settling back into a routine ever since Colleen had blown into their lives.

Convinced they'd overreacted, Frank started to turn away.

A sound made him pause.

A scurry of footsteps inside the room.

Before he could raise his hand to knock, Colleen's door opened.

Eyes wide. Hair in disarray. Lips still swollen with sleep.

"Someone's—" She gasped and pointed to the French doors. "Someone's on the back porch."

"Evie's bedroom is down the hall on the left. Stay with her. Lock the door. Don't let anyone in unless I tell you it's clear. Call 911 and notify the police."

She scurried past him.

"Come on, boy."

Duke followed him through the kitchen. Frank grabbed his Maglite and slipped outside, the dog at his side.

A breeze blew through the trees, the sound of rustling

leaves covering their footfalls. Frank's heart pounded. Trey wouldn't escape this time.

Gripping the Maglite in his left hand and his weapon in the right, Frank inched around the corner. A dark shadow, big and bulky, peered through the French doors into the room where Colleen had slept moments earlier.

At the same instant, sirens sounded in the distance.

The dark shadow turned and ran.

"Stop. Law enforcement."

The guy fled into the woods. Frank gave the command. Duke ran after him. Frank followed.

Shots fired.

Fearing Duke had been hit, Frank increased his pace and pushed harder.

The sound of a car engine filled the night. Tires screeched.

Frank whistled. The dog bounded from the wooded area.

Relieved to see his trusty friend unharmed, Frank slapped his leg. "Come on, boy."

They hurried back to the house. A police squad car pulled into the driveway.

"I didn't expect you to respond so quickly," Frank said to the cop who climbed from the car.

His name tag read Stoddard. He was tall and lean, midtwenties and blond. "I was in the area, sir."

Frank quickly filled him in on what he'd seen and heard.

Using the radio, Stoddard alerted other patrol cars. "The man is armed and dangerous."

While the officer examined the cut screen, Frank stepped inside and headed to Evelyn's room. He tapped on the door.

"It's Frank. You can come out. The guy ran off."

Evelyn threw open the door and gasped with relief when she saw Frank. “Colleen and I thought something had happened to you. We heard the shots and—”

He patted her shoulder. “The shots were aimed at Duke.”

Colleen looked alarmed. “Is he okay?”

“Seems to be fine.”

“Did you see the guy?” she asked.

“Only from the rear. He was wearing dark slacks and a hooded sweatshirt.”

“It was Trey.”

“We don’t know that for sure.”

The cop called from the front of the house. Evelyn tied her robe more tightly around her. “I’ll brew coffee.”

She hurried to the kitchen.

Colleen stepped closer. “Something woke me. I couldn’t recognize the sound at first. Looking out the window, I saw him cut through the screen.”

“Frank.” Evelyn’s voice. “The officer needs to ask you some questions.”

“He’ll want to talk to me, too,” Colleen said.

“I’ll stay with you.”

She nodded. “It’s okay. I don’t have anything to hide.”

The officer accepted a cup of coffee from Evelyn and took down the information that Frank and Colleen provided.

“Ma’am, did you recognize the prowler?” he eventually asked.

“I…I couldn’t tell who he was. It was dark. I don’t know if it was Trey Howard or someone else.”

“I’ll check with Officer Talbot, whom you spoke with at the hospital, and see if he’s uncovered anything new.”

“The officer said he’d issue a Bee Low,” she added.

Frank smiled. "That's BOLO. A Be On the Lookout order was sent to all law enforcement in the area."

The blond officer scratched his head. "Which I never received. I'll check that with Talbot, as well."

He glanced at Evelyn as he scooted back from the table and stood. "Thanks for the coffee, ma'am."

"I wish you'd take a slice of coffee cake for later."

He nodded his appreciation. "I'm training for a marathon next month and keeping my sugar to a minimum. But the coffee hit the spot."

Frank walked Stoddard to the front door and offered his hand. "Ms. Brennan's car is at the barn. See if your crime scene folks can get to it in the morning."

"I'll make that happen, sir."

The cop was young and seemed competent. Colleen had answered all the questions, but Frank wondered if she was holding something back.

Why did Trey keep coming after Colleen? Was it because of what she knew? Or did it involve more than a list of names and a photo?

There had to be something else that Trey wanted.

But what?

Just before Stoddard left the house, a car pulled into the driveway. While Colleen helped Evelyn tidy the kitchen, Frank opened the door, surprised to find Mayor Allen Quincy standing on the porch.

"Evening, Frank. Officer Stoddard." Tall, balding and wearing his fatigue, the mayor stepped into the foyer. He dropped his keys on a nearby table and shook both men's hands.

"Actually, sir," Stoddard said, "evening has long since passed. Everything okay?"

"Just doing a last-minute check in the Amish area."

Pulling a handkerchief from his pocket, the mayor wiped his forehead and smiled. “Age seems to be catching up with me.”

“I doubt that, sir,” Stoddard was quick to reply.

The mayor smiled. “I saw your squad car when I drove by. The dispatcher said there was a break-in.”

“An attempted break-in,” Frank explained. “The guy got as far as the screened-in porch.”

The mayor shook his head with regret, his shoulders sagging ever so slightly. “We’ve had vandalism in the trailer park that was hit by the tornado. I had hoped the Amish area wouldn’t have that problem.”

Evelyn wiped her hands on a towel and joined the men in the foyer. “Care for a cup of coffee, Allen?”

“Thanks, Evelyn, but I’ll take a rain check.”

Another knock. “Seems everyone’s stopping by tonight.” Frank opened the door.

A second police officer stood on the porch with his hand on the shoulder of a young Amish boy.

“Evening, Mayor. Ma’am. Sir.” He peered through the crowd at Colleen and nodded to her, as well.

“I hate to bother you folks this late,” the officer said, “but I found this young man walking through your property. I wanted to see if you could identify him as your prowler.”

Colleen stared at the Amish lad. “You were behind the barn when the wall came down.”

The boy tensed. “I did nothing wrong.”

“What about tonight, son?” Frank asked. “What were you doing this far from home, especially so late?”

Evelyn reached for the boy’s hand. “Isaac, it’s good to see you. Was Mr. Malone tutoring you? Did you have a night session?”

The boy shook his head. "I…I was talking to Lucy Wyatt."

"Marsha and Carter Wyatt's daughter?"

"*Jah.* They are her parents."

Evelyn looked at the two officers and the mayor. "I can vouch for Isaac. He works at the Craft Shoppe and selects the best produce and baked goods for me. He's a fine young man."

Recalling the bulk of the guy on the porch, Frank had to agree with his sister. "The intruder was taller and more filled out."

He turned to Isaac. "Did you see anyone in the woods when you were with Lucy?"

The Amish boy shook his head. "No one."

The mayor checked his watch. "I'm headed back your way, Isaac. I'll take you home."

He hung his head. "My *dat* does not know I left the house."

The mayor thought for a moment and then patted the boy's shoulder. "Then we won't tell him. I'll drop you at the end of your driveway. He won't hear my car."

Turning to the officer still standing on the porch, the mayor asked, "Does that meet with your approval?"

"Yes, sir. No need for me to file a report as long as you're taking the boy home."

"Thanks for your hospitality, Evelyn."

"Anytime, Mayor."

As he turned to leave, Colleen pointed to the keys on the foyer table. A plastic picture frame was attached to the chain.

Frank followed her gaze and stared at the photo of a young woman in a wedding dress.

The mayor patted his pocket and then laughed as he

reached for the forgotten keys. “Isaac and I wouldn’t have gotten far without these.”

“The photo?” Colleen asked.

“That’s my daughter.” The mayor beamed with pride. “She got married in Atlanta last summer and gave the key chain with the attached picture to me for Christmas.”

“She used an Atlanta photographer?”

“That’s right. He seemed like a nice guy. My daughter was happy with the photos, so that’s all that matters.”

Once everyone left, Frank closed and locked the door. “A busy place tonight.”

Evelyn shook her head with regret. “I fear Isaac’s heart is going to be broken.”

“Oh?”

“Lucy Wyatt is not Amish.”

Evelyn returned to the kitchen.

Colleen’s eyes were wide. She grabbed Frank’s hand. “The bride’s picture had the name of the photographer written in the corner.”

Frank knew before she told him.

“The photographer was Trey Howard.”

THIRTEEN

Colleen woke the next morning and stretched out her hand to pet Duke. Frank had insisted the dog stay in her room throughout the night. She had slept soundly knowing the German shepherd was standing guard.

"You're such a good dog." Duke lifted his ears and tilted his head, letting her rub behind his ears and pat his neck. "Thanks for taking care of me last night."

She glanced at the clock and groaned—9:00 a.m. She'd slept later than she wanted. At first, she'd tossed and turned while reviewing the questions the police officer had asked. True to his word, Frank had sat next to her and filled in any blanks when she got stuck on an answer. Evelyn had stayed up and encouraged them to eat the cake and cookies she served, never appearing fazed by Frank's explanation about Trey and his drug operation.

The arrival of the Amish boy and the mayor added to her concern, especially when she'd seen Trey's name on the key-chain photo. Surely the mayor wasn't involved in a drug operation, yet the coincidence added to her unease.

Crawling from bed, Colleen quickly showered and changed into jeans and a pullover top. The memory card was weighing heavily on her mind.

Hurrying into the kitchen, her enthusiasm plummeted when she found a note from Evelyn on the counter. "I have to work at the library for a few hours. I'll be home in time for lunch."

Knowing Frank was probably at the triage site, Colleen glanced out the kitchen window, searching for a glimpse of him in the valley below. Hopefully Evelyn wouldn't be gone too long. Feeling a bit skittish at being alone, she rubbed her hands over her arms and tried to still her growing anxiety.

Duke stood at the front door and barked. Of course, she wasn't alone. She had a wonderful guard dog.

"Sorry, boy, I wasn't thinking of you."

She let him out and returned to the kitchen to brew coffee. Evelyn had left coffee cake on the counter with a second note. "Help yourself. Eggs and bacon are in the fridge. Homemade bread is next to the stove."

She smiled, grateful for Evelyn's hospitality.

As the coffee dripped, Colleen hurried back to check on Duke.

Footsteps sounded on the front porch.

She stopped short. Her stomach tightened. She hadn't completely closed the door. Through the cracked opening, she saw a man, wearing jeans and a black sweater.

Heart in her throat, she backed into the kitchen and grabbed a knife from the wooden butcher block by the stove. Holding it close to her side, she mentally outlined her options.

How much protection would the knife provide?

Not enough.

She needed help.

She needed Frank.

"Colleen?"

Frank's voice. She gasped with relief and felt foolish for thinking Frank could possibly be Trey. She dropped the knife on the table and tried to blink back tears, but she couldn't stop the rush of emotion that swept over her.

Frank's face was twisted with concern. He opened his arms, and she fell into his embrace.

Her control broke. She sobbed, unable to stop the onslaught. She had been so strong for so long. She'd stood by her dying sister and promised she'd bring Trey to justice, but she hadn't been able to gather enough evidence or convince law enforcement of his guilt.

No one believed her. Not even Frank.

Until now.

Much as she didn't want to admit the truth, Colleen felt responsible for her sister's death. She'd been so determined to show Briana tough love that she'd failed to respond to her plea for help.

Why hadn't she been more sensitive, more caring, more who Christ wanted her to be? Maybe because she'd been burned by Briana so many times in the past. Still, that wasn't reason to forsake her sister in a time of need.

Frank pulled her closer. His hand rubbed over her shoulders. Lips close to her ear, he whispered soothing words that were like a lifeline to a drowning woman.

"Shh, Colleen, I've got you. I won't let anyone hurt you."

"I...I thought you were—"

"I'm sorry for scaring you. I went out to get the morning paper. When I saw Duke, I wanted to make sure you were okay."

She nodded and wiped her cheeks, concentrating on Frank's strength and the understanding so evident in his voice.

"I...I closed my heart to Briana." The words came unbidden. She had to admit her mistake.

"It's okay, honey."

"She had nowhere else to turn except to Trey."

"Even with your help, she probably would have gone back to him. The statistics aren't good for anyone hooked on drugs. Without rehab, without the will to make a change—"

"Without God," Colleen added, her lips trembling.

"That's it exactly. As much as you wanted Briana to walk away from her addiction, she couldn't, and you couldn't do it for her. She went to Trey, not because of you, but because of her need for drugs."

"If only she hadn't gotten involved with him."

"Where'd they meet?"

"I'm not sure. She worked at the King's Club for almost two years. It's in the heart of the city and known to have the wrong type of clientele. Trey may have been a regular. I told her it was a bad place. I don't know if she quit the job because of me or if she got tired of what she saw."

"Did she know the two women who died?"

"She never mentioned them. The last time she phoned wanting money, I said no. She overdosed a few days later."

Colleen looked into Frank's dark eyes, which reflected the pain she was carrying.

"I have to stop Trey. That's the promise I made to Briana."

He nodded. "I'm in this with you. We'll get him. He won't hurt anyone again."

"There's…there's something else I have to tell you."

Frank tensed ever so slightly.

She felt the change, but she couldn't stop now. Everything needed to be revealed.

"When I entered Trey's office, I was searching for evidence that would convince the police. I told you about the picture on his screen."

Frank nodded. "Go on."

"That night, Trey was using an external card reader to view his digital photographs from a memory card. I needed more evidence, so I took the card, although I never had time to look at the pictures."

"He must have realized the memory card was gone. Didn't he come after you?"

"He sent one of his men to my apartment later that night. I was scheduled on a flight early the next morning. My carry-on was packed so I left through a back door, made my flight the next day and then checked into a motel when I got back to Atlanta. That's when the gal who lived across the hall called me. She said someone else had been snooping around."

"You thought that was Anderson, the cop from Atlanta."

"I'm not sure. Anderson or one of Trey's men. Soon after that, I called Vivian. She had evidence that would prove Trey's involvement. At least that's what she told me."

"The video."

"She didn't tell me what she had, but she did ask what type of phone I used."

"Why didn't you tell me before about the memory card?"

"Trey took my photograph with a couple of the men who worked for him. I didn't want to be in the picture, but he insisted. If I made too much of it, I knew he'd get suspicious."

"What's that have to do with not telling me?"

"I…I wasn't sure how you'd react if you saw me with the men. You didn't believe me earlier. The photo wouldn't have improved my credibility, especially if they were known drug traffickers. Plus, I worried Trey might have doctored the photo to incriminate me even more. Guilt by association, they call it, but I'm innocent of any wrongdoing."

She glanced up, and her breath hitched. "Do you believe me, Frank?"

"Why wouldn't I?" His voice was flat and his eyes had lost their spark of interest. He was trying to cover up his true feelings.

"Where's the memory card now?" He took a step back, distancing himself from her.

She shook her head, struggling to control a second wave of tears that threatened. Frank didn't believe her.

"It was in my purse. The contents were strewn under the seat in the storm. I'm sure it's still in the car."

"I'll check it out."

He started to turn away from her. She grabbed his arm. "I'm going with you."

She'd ride to the triage area with Frank. Hopefully they'd find the memory card, but then she'd leave Freemont and go someplace safe.

She never wanted Trey or his men to find her.

She didn't want Frank to find her either.

A stiff breeze blew as Frank pulled out of Evelyn's driveway. He'd left Duke behind, but Colleen sat next to him, her arms crossed and her shoulders straight.

Frank had been attracted to Colleen and ready to go the distance for her. Then she mentioned the memory card, which was another bit of evidence she had kept from him.

He didn't understand her or her actions.

She wanted Trey stopped, yet she refused to share

crucial information with him. Didn't she trust him to be an effective investigator?

After his injury, he hadn't been enough of a man for Audrey. Evidently he wasn't enough of an investigator for Colleen.

He remembered the way she had felt in his arms. Truth be told, he hadn't wanted to let her go. Instead, he wanted to protect her and do whatever he could to stop her tears and bring joy to her life.

He hadn't felt that way with Audrey. Their relationship had been surface, which Audrey had made blatantly clear when she'd walked away. Too late he realized the truth. Frank had being drawn to Audrey by her outward looks, not by an inner beauty.

Colleen was beautiful inside and out, but it wasn't her looks that attracted him to her. It was her focus, her strength and her need to right the wrong that drugs had caused her sister. Frank knew that drive. It's why he had joined the military and eventually transferred to the CID. He wanted to right wrongs and help those in need.

If only he could explain his feelings to Colleen, but she was centered on finding the memory card and bringing Trey to justice. No reason to mix personal relationships with an investigation. He knew better, even if Colleen had pulled him off course.

He drove down the hill faster than he should have and braked to a stop beside the barn.

"Where's my car?" Colleen demanded, the first comment she'd made since climbing into his truck at his sister's house.

"Stay here."

"I will not." She threw open the door and jumped down. "What did you do with my Honda?"

"Nothing."

"Did the local cops impound the car?"

"I'll find out."

Frank pulled his cell from his pocket and called the Freemont PD. He asked to speak with Officer Stoddard.

"I told you about the car buried in debris in the barn," Frank said when Stoddard came on the line.

"Yes, sir."

"Did your crime scene team check it out?"

"Ah, I'm not sure. Give me a minute."

Frank waited, his frustration rising.

"Sir." Stoddard returned. "Our crime scene team scheduled the Honda for late afternoon."

"That would work except the car is gone."

"Gone?"

"Exactly. Someone's taken the car, and I want it found."

"Yes, sir."

Frank disconnected. "The cops don't know what happened," he told Colleen.

"Someone does."

A horse and buggy clip-clopped along the road. Frank flagged down the bearded farmer. He wore a light blue shirt and a straw hat that nearly covered his eyes. A teenage boy, clean-shaven and similarly dressed, sat next to him.

"Mr. Fisher?"

"Whoa, there. Whoa." He pulled his horse to a stop.

Frank pointed to the barn. "There was a car in that barn. Do you know where it's been taken?"

The Amish man shook his head.

Frank turned to the teen. "What about you, Isaac? Did you do anything to the car?"

The bearded man bristled. "Why do you ask this of my son?"

Holding up his hand, Frank said, "Sir, let him answer the question."

"A bulldozer was in the area." The teen pointed across the street to the construction worker clearing debris around the farmhouse. "Ask that man."

Frank nodded his thanks and waited until the buggy had passed before he hurried across the street.

Spotting his approach, the driver shoved the gear in Neutral and allowed the bulldozer to idle in place.

"Paul, isn't it?" The guy who had worked around the barn yesterday.

He nodded. "That's right. Paul Yates."

"What happened to the car that was in the barn?" Frank pointed back to where Colleen stood staring at the ground.

"Someone loaded it on a flatbed." Paul rubbed his chin. "Junkyard Jack? Junkyard Jason? Seems it started with the letter *J*."

"Junkyard Joe's."

The guy nodded. "That's it."

"Who authorized the pickup?" Probably a long shot to think the Atlanta construction worker would know, but no harm asking.

"No clue about authorization, but the guy in charge of the whole cleanup was talking to the driver of the flatbed. Someone said he was the mayor."

"Allen Quincy. Did you see anyone else?"

"Just the two guys from the junkyard."

Frank nodded his thanks and hustled back to Colleen, who was picking through the hay and debris.

"I'm checking the ground in case the memory card ended up outside the car," she explained as he neared. "When the twister hit, my only thought was staying alive."

"Find anything?"

"Lots of stuff. No memory card. Any luck on your end?"

"Seems the mayor may have gotten carried away with his cleanup campaign and had your car hauled off to the local junkyard."

"That's our next stop?"

He nodded. "But first, let's give this area a thorough search so we don't have to backtrack."

Frank worked back and forth, in a grid-like pattern, just as he had been trained to do with crime scene investigations. Colleen walked beside him, and both of them seemed satisfied when they left in Frank's pickup forty-five minutes later.

"Junkyard Joe's sits on the other side of town," Frank said. "I'll give you a tour of Freemont on the way."

He turned off Amish Road and headed due east, first through a residential area that had escaped damage and then along a country lane.

"Such a beautiful area." She took in the rolling hills and sprawling farms that stretched on each side of the roadway.

A newer home with an expansive back deck was visible in the distance, situated on a road that ran parallel of the one they traveled.

"Dawson Timmons, a former CID agent, lives there." Frank pointed to the house and surrounding farmland. "He got out of the army, married a local girl, bought land and started farming. They're nice folks who go to Evelyn's church."

"But you don't?"

Frank glanced at her. "Don't go to church?"

She nodded.

"I haven't yet. Maybe one of these days."

Silent for a long moment, Colleen finally spoke. "I didn't think much about religion until my sister died. Since then I've tried to do better, but I haven't joined a church."

"You were busy tracking down Trey."

"Looking back, I realize trying to take him down by myself was probably a mistake."

"It's fairly obvious you don't trust law enforcement."

There, he'd stated the major obstacle that stood between them. She didn't trust anyone with a badge, yet she couldn't achieve her goal without law enforcement's help.

"Not all of us are on the take, Colleen."

"As I recall, you have trust issues, too." Her voice was tight, her focus still on the road.

"Because I question information that can't be substantiated?"

"Because you don't believe me."

He pulled in a ragged breath. He wanted to believe Colleen. When he looked into her eyes, he saw a good woman who was trying to do what was right, but he had this fear of not making the right decision or seeing things the way they really were.

Was that holding him back?

"It's not personal."

She harrumphed. "You've talked yourself into thinking you're doing what's right, yet you can't see the truth."

"The truth about—"

"The truth about me. I'm trying to gather enough evidence to put Trey Howard in jail for life. You and I are actually on the same side of the law. The problem is you're always questioning your own ability and your compromised strength and your weakened condition."

Did he appear weak to her?

"You think your injury and infection affected your

investigative skills," she continued, hardly pausing long enough to take a breath. "You're still the man you were before, Frank. You're still a CID agent able to track down evidence and bring the guilty to justice. You just lack confidence. You're looking back at what happened in Afghanistan and during your long hospitalization. It must have been difficult, but you've healed. You're ready to get back to work, to embrace life fully."

She sighed. "You're the same man, only maybe a bit more cautious and more aware of your own mortality. That's not a bad thing. Sometimes when we think we can do it all ourselves, we forget about God. But we can't do anything without Him. Allow Him into your brokenness, and you'll be able to heal."

He hesitated for a long moment. Then pulling in a deep breath, he asked, "What about you, Colleen? Have you healed?"

She shook her head. "I still can't get over losing Briana. Much as I want to believe the tough love was for her own good, I keep wondering if it led to her death. If only I'd opened my heart and brought her back into my life, I could have taken care of her. I could have loved her. I could have helped her battle her addiction."

"She needed rehab."

Colleen shook her head. "She'd been to rehab. It hadn't stopped her from finding drugs."

"Chances are she wouldn't have done anything different the second time. Drug addiction is like quicksand. She couldn't free herself even if she wanted to, and you couldn't have pulled her out. It's not easy to realize drugs have such control over someone we love, but it's the truth. She loved drugs more than she loved herself."

"More than she loved me," Colleen whispered.

Frank didn't know anything else he could say that

would ease Colleen's guilt or assuage her grief. If Trey had been guilty of drug trafficking, he needed to be stopped so that no other woman was sucked into the downward spiral of addiction. The addict wasn't the only one affected. The entire family was, as well.

Colleen was proof of that.

She deserved more than heartbreak over a sister's dependence on cocaine. Colleen deserved to be loved and accepted. If only she would lower the wall she had raised around her heart.

Frank didn't know how to change her opinion of law enforcement, but he wanted her future to be bright. He was beginning to think being part of her future might be good for him, as well.

FOURTEEN

A musty smell wafted past Colleen and mixed with the haze of dust and the cloying scent of rusted metal when they drove into the junkyard. Stepping out of the pickup, she tried to hold her breath but quickly ran out of air.

"Are you okay?" Frank asked.

"I'm fine." Which she wasn't. Her head ached, and she was tired of arguing about trust and the lack thereof.

A man left the ramshackle shack that served as an office and headed to a Ford 4x4 parked nearby. The truck looked new.

"Joe?" Frank waved to the guy as he opened the door and started to climb behind the wheel.

Evidently the owner. Joe looked as scruffy as his junkyard, although his truck was pristine. Untrimmed beard, long hair pulled into a ponytail topped with a baseball hat. His name was embroidered on the front chest pocket of his work shirt.

"You need something?" he called back to them.

"A blue Honda injured in the tornado. You or a couple of your workers picked it up this morning." Frank held up his CID badge.

"They unloaded in the west end." Joe pointed them in the right direction. "Head along the path around the mound of old parts. You'll see the Honda."

Frank reached for Colleen's hand. She hadn't expected his grip to be so strong.

"Let's go."

She hurried after him.

Passing the pile of car parts and twisted metal, she groaned when the expansive west end, as Joe had called it, came into view. The junkyard extended for acres. "This might take some time."

Two paths wove through a graveyard of discarded cars. Doors hung open. The hoods on many of the vehicles were raised, allowing engines to rust from the elements. Trunks were cocked at odd angles. Birds perched on the bottom rims pecked at bugs that lived in the shaded interior.

Colleen glanced at the ground, expecting to see vermin underfoot.

Frank squeezed her hand.

"I'm imagining rats and other creatures," she admitted.

"We'll make noise to scare away anything on four legs."

"What about the two-legged vermin?"

"I'll watch for them, as well."

Trey would do anything to save himself and his profitable drug operation. Colleen stood in his way.

He'd tried to kill her before. He'd try again.

She glanced at Frank's hand that still held hers.

He didn't believe her, yet Frank was helping her find the memory card. Probably because he needed the evidence that would end Trey's hateful abuse of the women he trafficked and the men and women—many young kids who didn't make good decisions—who used the drugs he brought illegally into the United States.

He had to be stopped.

Frank would help her bring Trey to justice. He'd also work to keep her safe, but once he had the digital memory card, he'd no longer need Colleen.

She dropped his hand and started down one of two paths winding through the rows of cars.

Colleen had to rely on her own ability, her own strength. She'd made a mistake letting her guard down around Frank. A mistake she already regretted. At least she hadn't made an even bigger mistake by giving him her heart.

Frank didn't know why he had taken Colleen's hand, especially after the tension that had sparked between them earlier.

He blamed it on his protective nature when he was around her. An inner voice kept warning him to be alert to danger.

Joe was a typical redneck who ran a fairly profitable business despite his scrubby beard and ponytail. The junkyard was a fixture in Freemont, and even Evelyn gave her stamp of approval when Frank had called her and mentioned Joe's name.

Still, something niggled within Frank, a nervous anxiety that had him looking over his shoulder and wanting to keep Colleen close by his side.

She, on the other hand, had charged off in one direction to cover more area, while he followed on the neighboring path.

He cupped his hands around his mouth. "See anything?"

She shook her head. "A lot of junk but no blue Honda."

Frank spotted an old woody station wagon, a Studebaker and other makes and models that had to be classics by now. Some of them could be refurbished into a decent ride, for the right price.

That was the point. No one would spend hard-earned cash for a rusty car that had been exposed to the elements. Joe made money by selling parts, which left the cars picked over like roadkill.

His eyes scanned rows of automobiles, trucks, even a couple of buses and an RV that had all seen better days. Some had been plucked clean. Others sat seemingly untouched in the afternoon sun.

The two paths came together up ahead. In the distance, Frank noted movement on a small hill that formed a natural end to Joe's acreage.

He squinted, trying to determine what he'd seen. A gust of wind stirred trees on the gentle slope. Surely that's what had diverted his attention.

He glanced over his shoulder, ensuring they weren't being followed.

Turning back to the hill, he focused on a narrow dirt path, barely wide enough for a compact car.

"Something wrong?" Colleen asked.

"Just checking the area."

"I see a blue car just beyond the fork where the two paths meet."

Frank followed her gaze. "Looks like your Honda."

He hurried to meet up with her.

The Honda sat behind a wall of vehicles.

"How do we crawl through all that wreckage?" she asked.

"We'll go around some of the cars and over others." He glanced at her feet, glad to see she was wearing shoes with rubber soles.

"Let me check it out. You stay on the path."

She shook her head, just as he'd known she would. "We go together."

"You could twist an ankle or get cut on a piece of metal."

She nodded. "That's a risk I'll take. Plus, I could offer the same warning to you."

"Shall I lead then?"

"Be my guest."

Frank climbed onto the hood of a four-door sedan and offered Colleen his hand. She put her foot on the front bumper, and he helped her up to where he stood. The hood buckled. "Watch your step."

He leaped to the next car and reached for her as she followed. "Two more cars to go."

They crawled across the front seat of a third car and inched their way around a fourth to reach the Honda.

Frank jerked open the driver's door. Colleen looked under the front seat. "The memory card was in my purse."

"Did anything else fall out?"

She nodded. "Everything, including my wallet and lipstick." She patted the floorboard and shook her head when she came up empty-handed. "Maybe it's in the backseat."

"Watch out for broken glass," Frank cautioned.

She searched the rear, but found nothing.

With a sigh, she extracted herself. "It's not there."

"Let me try."

She stepped back to give him room. Bending down, he tugged at the carpet. Two sections were attached by Velcro. Pulling the rug away from the floorboard, he smiled, seeing a small square card.

Grabbing it, he started to stand.

"Look what—"

A shot pinged against the car.

Colleen screamed.

He grasped her shoulders and shoved her down, protecting her body with his own.

Reaching for the Glock on his hip, he glared at the hill and the narrow path where he'd seen movement.

Another ping. Glass exploded as the shot hit the window of the car behind them.

"It's Trey, isn't it?" Colleen cried.

"At this point it doesn't matter who's shooting at us. We need to get out of here."

Frank pulled his cell phone free. He called 911 and relayed the information to the operator. "Tell the police to get here now."

A narrow path led toward a rusted school bus that offered better protection.

"Keep low."

More shots followed them.

"Are you hurt?" Frank asked, once they were behind the bus.

Fear flashed from her eyes, but she shook her head. "I'm okay."

He peered around the corner of the bus and studied the hillside.

Movement. A man aimed a rifle.

Frank raised his Glock and fired three shots.

The guy ducked into the underbrush.

Glancing behind him, Frank searched for another exit. Leaving the protection of the bus would put them in the shooter's sights.

Another volley of fire. A bus window shattered. Frank threw himself over Colleen to shield her from the falling shards.

"Stay down," he warned again.

Frank stared at the hillside. The breeze blew the trees,

but a bush moved in the opposite direction. The guy was trying to escape.

Frank took aim and squeezed the trigger.

Sirens sounded in the distance.

He fired again.

The police cars rolled into the junkyard. Four cops jumped from their sedans, weapons drawn, and raced to the bus.

Frank quickly filled them in and pointed to the hill.

Another police car circled around the perimeter of the junkyard and raced up the slope. The cop screeched to a stop and took cover as he climbed from his vehicle. After a quick search, he raised his hand and shook his head.

Behind Frank, an officer spoke into his radio. "The area's clear?"

Static squawked.

"Roger that. Looks like our shooter left before we arrived."

He stepped to where Frank helped Colleen to her feet.

"The shooter took off, sir. We'll set up roadblocks. You were looking for something in the blue Honda?"

"That's correct. He must have followed us."

"We've got a BOLO out on Trey Howard. I'll notify you if we spot the suspect."

Frank took Colleen's hand and helped her back to his truck.

She looked exhausted and scared. He put his arm around her shoulders.

"We'll get him," he kept saying, although he didn't think she believed him.

"He wants to kill me," she whispered, her voice thick.

"You saw him shoot Vivian. He doesn't want you to testify against him. He may plan to escape to that Colombian resort he told you about."

"You can't let him leave the country." She grabbed Frank's hand.

"I'll have CID contact the airlines in Atlanta and the surrounding areas, Birmingham, Jacksonville, Nashville. He won't leave by air. At least not if we can help it."

She rested her head against his shoulder and sighed. "If only we'd found the memory chip, then we'd have proof. All I wanted was enough evidence to see him behind bars."

"I found it, Colleen."

"The memory card?"

He nodded.

She grabbed his hand, pried it open and found it empty. She stared up at him, perplexed and almost angry. "I'm not laughing if you think teasing me is funny."

"Trust me," he said as he dug into his pants pocket and pulled out the memory card.

"Oh, Frank, you found it. Now you can arrest Trey and try him for drug trafficking."

Frank looked at the hill where two additional police cars now searched for any clue that would lead them to the shooter.

To Colleen it all seemed so simple. They had the evidence. The photos along with Vivian's testimony would be enough to try him and hopefully find him guilty in a court of law.

But finding Trey was the challenge.

Even with the mounting police effort, he could elude the roadblocks. If he left the country, they'd never bring him to justice.

The old Frank wouldn't have felt discouraged, but the injured Frank—the one who was still out of shape—didn't know who would win in the end.

FIFTEEN

"Go on, Frank," Colleen said once they were back at Evelyn's house. "You need to take the memory card to CID Headquarters. Show it to Colby. I'm sure Special Agent in Charge Wilson will be interested, as well."

"We could look at the photos here on my computer, and then email them to Wilson," he suggested.

"Doesn't he need the evidence in hand?"

Frank nodded but still hesitated.

"Your sister and I both insist you get going," Colleen continued. "We'll be fine. Duke will protect us if anyone unsavory comes around."

"Trey's on the loose. He knows you're here."

"And didn't police notify you that the highway patrol apprehended a man who fit his description?" Evelyn interjected.

"His identify hasn't been verified yet."

"Maybe not," Colleen said with a sigh, "but he was stopped on the interstate, heading to Atlanta, soon after the shooting at Junkyard Joe's. The rifle in his car had recently been shot. It all adds up, Frank."

"Except he claims to have been hunting earlier today."

"You two can keep arguing." Evelyn picked up the telephone. "I'm calling Ron and asking him to stay with us while you're gone."

She raised her brow at her brother. "Will that convince you that we'll be safe?"

"Does Ron know how to use a gun?"

"He served in the military and goes hunting with his uncle. The awards hanging in his office attest to his marksmanship."

Frank nodded. "Tell him I'll leave a weapon in the top drawer of my dresser. It'll be loaded, just in case."

Evelyn passed on the information to Ron after he accepted the invitation to visit.

She hung up with a smile. "He considers it an honor to defend two lovely women."

Colleen ignored the niggling concern she still had about Ron, and instead smiled at the twinkle in Evelyn's eyes. She was lucky to have someone who cared for her.

Feeling a tug at her heart, Colleen glanced at Frank, wishing things could be different between them. He was a good and caring man and a good investigator even after the medical problems he'd undergone.

The way he talked about the military and the CID, he was ready to return to active duty. Maybe Special Agent in Charge Wilson would say he was needed now.

Peering out the kitchen window, Colleen stared at the cleanup and reconstruction going on along Amish Road. The collapsed structures and downed trees had been cleared and either piled at the edge of the road or already transported to the town landfill and dump.

Frank came up behind her and touched her arm. "You're okay with me going?"

"Of course." She wouldn't tell him about the tingle of concern that had her rubbing her arms and asking for the Lord's protection.

Trey was probably already in custody.

Pulling in a cleansing breath, she smiled. Frank had a

newfound energy and enthusiasm in his step. Going back to work would be just what the doctor ordered.

"Don't worry," she insisted. "We'll be fine."

"I won't be long."

He looked at Duke, lying in the corner. "Stay. Take care of Colleen and Evelyn."

Duke tilted his head as if he understood.

"Frank," Colleen called after him, "be safe."

But he'd already left the house.

Frank headed toward town and River Road, which would take him to post. Colleen was right. He and Colby needed to go over the photos on the memory card. The authorities in Atlanta would have to be notified. DEA would also be interested in what they uncovered.

His cell rang. "Special Agent Gallagher."

"Sir, this is Officer Stoddard, Freemont PD. I notified you that Georgia Highway Patrol pulled over a white male wearing a red plaid shirt."

"That's right. Trey Howard. Is he in custody?"

"Not yet, sir. They need someone to ID him."

Frank had seen him in the hospital and on the video. "Give me directions."

Five miles north of Freemont on the interstate. The detour wouldn't take long. "I'm headed there now."

Frank disconnected and increased his speed. Knowing Trey would soon be in custody gave Frank a sense of satisfaction. Working on the case felt good. Knowing Trey wouldn't be able to draw others into his drug world was even better.

Frank would like to tell the guy a thing or two, in a professional way, of course. Then he'd drive to post and drop off the memory chip. Colby could do the initial review of the pictures while he hurried back to be with Colleen.

Was he crazy to be attracted to a woman who didn't trust law enforcement? Probably, but he'd never taken the easy route in life, and right now, he wanted to tell her how she made him feel.

After Frank left the house, Colleen tried to convince herself that everything was working out just the way she had wanted. Trey had been apprehended, but she was unsettled by a sense of concern she couldn't shake. She wandered back to the kitchen, where Evelyn was washing dishes.

Reaching for a dish towel, Colleen stepped toward the sink. "Mind if I dry?"

"No need, unless you want something to do."

Evelyn had a knack for knowing what was on Colleen's mind. "Frank's ready to get back to work."

"He's been ready for some time, although his strength needed to improve." Evelyn sighed. "The explosion in Afghanistan was traumatic enough, but he had to face the surgeries in Landstuhl and then more at Walter Reed and in Augusta. He wanted to move on with his life."

She ran more hot water in the sink. "Did he tell you about Audrey?"

Colleen shook her head. "We haven't discussed personal matters. Usually we're talking about Trey." And struggling with trust issues, which she didn't mentioned.

"Frank doesn't talk about the past to me either. It's as if he wants to bury the memories with the rubble that buried him in Afghanistan."

Colleen dried a glass and placed it in the cabinet, waiting for Evelyn to continue.

"He dated Audrey before his unit deployed. Frank thought she'd wait for him."

"They were good together?" Colleen asked.

"Frank thought so."

"But you didn't agree?"

"What do sisters know?" Evelyn shrugged. "I didn't tell Frank, but Audrey seemed more interested in having a handsome guy on her arm than being with Frank."

Colleen nodded, thinking of Briana's attraction for wealth and power and surface attractions.

"When Audrey left him, Frank tried to shrug off the hurt, then the infection set in. At one point, I feared he'd lose the will to live."

"That doesn't sound like Frank."

"He lost so much weight. He was on a ventilator. His kidneys started to shut down. The doctors didn't give me much hope."

"I'm sure you kept praying."

Evelyn nodded. "I prayed. Ron prayed. The whole church community prayed. His recovery was slow and hard, but Frank turned the corner, although he's still testing his own ability as if he's not quite sure of himself."

"He's stronger than he realizes. He'll be fine."

"Maybe, but he needs a good woman to encourage him."

"I doubt Frank thinks he needs anyone's help."

"Maybe not, but he does. I see the way he looks at you."

Colleen's breath hitched. "What do you mean?"

"You touch a spot in him. Someplace he's kept hidden. You've been a good influence."

She shook her head. "The only thing I've done is cause problems."

"That's not true. You've made him interested in life again."

Taken aback by Evelyn's comment, Colleen searched for a way to change the subject. "Ron seems like a great guy."

She nodded. "I'm very thankful he came into my life. He's everything Dan wasn't."

Colleen reached for another glass. "Is there something you want to talk about?"

Evelyn nodded. "How to tell Ron. He needs to know the truth about a guy I dated and thought was Mr. Right. I believed all his sweet talk and was naive to think our relationship would lead to marriage."

"Dan didn't feel the same way?"

"He invited me to meet him at a nearby state park for a late-afternoon picnic lunch. Of course, I expected something special. Storm clouds hovered overhead, but I didn't let that dampen my enthusiasm. Only Dan didn't plan to propose. He wanted to soothe his conscience and tell me about his wife and three children."

"Oh, Evelyn, I'm so sorry."

"I had no idea. He'd been so good at keeping everything secret, and I hadn't seen through his duplicity."

"What happened?"

"I railed at him. Told him he was despicable for what he'd done to his family as well as me. I told him I never wanted to see him again."

Evelyn sighed, and the weight of her upset was still evident. "The storm hit as I left the park. The road was slick. Visibility was bad. I was driving much too fast and didn't make one of the curves."

"The accident that hurt your leg. Frank told me he came home to help you."

"I was too embarrassed to tell him about Dan or the

reason for the accident. Growing up, Frank never struggled with relationships. He had lots of girlfriends over the years. He was tall and strong and handsome. I was always the sister no one noticed."

Colleen knew the feeling. "That's a hard place to be."

"I love Frank. He's got a heart of gold, but he needs to find God and learn what's important in life. As much as I hated to see him suffer through all those operations and the infection, they've opened his eyes. He realizes he can't take care of everything. If only he would start relying on God."

"You're a good influence on him, Evelyn."

"Which is what I said about you." She laughed. "Maybe we both have a positive effect on him."

"And Ron?"

"I want to tell him about Dan, but I'm not sure how he'll react."

"Ron cares deeply for you, Evelyn. He'll understand."

"I hope so." Evelyn checked her watch. "Wonder what's keeping him. He was ready to leave the house when I called. The drive only takes a few minutes."

"He's probably on the way."

"I'm going to phone just to be safe."

Safe. That's what Colleen wanted. She wanted Trey behind bars so she wouldn't have to worry anymore or look over her shoulder to see if she was being followed.

"Ron?" Evelyn held the phone close to her ear. Her voice held more than a note of concern. "You don't sound well. Tell me what happened."

So there had been a problem.

Colleen finished drying the dishes. She didn't want to eavesdrop, but the tremble in Evelyn's voice was worrisome.

"I'm coming over." Evelyn's face was pale and her hand shook as she disconnected.

She grabbed the keys to her car and her purse. "I have to hurry. Ron blacked out earlier. He came to feeling queasy and weak. You'll be okay?"

"Of course. Don't worry about me."

"Pray for Ron," Evelyn said as she left the house.

Lord, help Ron. Don't let anything happen to him.

Colleen locked the door and called Duke.

No reason for her to be worried about her own safety. She wasn't alone. Duke would protect her. At least, she hoped he would.

Frank drove hurriedly through town and headed for I-75, the interstate that stretched from Florida to Atlanta and then farther north into Tennessee.

Two miles outside Freemont, he spied a gathering of highway patrol cars parked on the side of the interstate. Their lights flashed, warning motorists to move to the far lane and give them a wide berth.

Frank braked to a stop and parked behind a Freemont police cruiser. Before exiting his car, he called Colleen.

"You're okay?" he asked when she answered. With a growing concern for her well-being, he feared leaving had been a mistake.

"I'm fine. Where are you?"

"Parked on the side of the interstate with the highway patrol. They want me to ID Trey."

Frank had planned to visit CID Headquarters next, but he felt a sudden need to change his plans. "I'll stop by the house on my way to Fort Rickman."

"You don't have to worry."

"I want to ensure you're safe," he said before he disconnected.

Crawling from his truck, he flashed his badge to the closest officer and introduced himself. "Freemont police called. You've apprehended a possible suspect in a shooting?"

The cop nodded. "His rifle's been fired recently. We received the BOLO. The latest update said he could be wearing a red plaid shirt."

Frank nodded. "Take me to him."

The officer led the way through a swarm of uniforms. Twenty feet from the road, a man sat on the ground, hands cuffed behind his back.

"Who's in charge?" Frank asked.

The officer pointed to a big guy wearing a highway patrol uniform and a Smokey Bear hat. Again Frank showed his badge and provided his name.

"Trey Howard shot a military wife at a roadside park near Freemont. Army CID is working the investigation," he quickly filled in.

"Can you ID the guy?" the patrolman asked. "His driver's license says he's Vince Lawson."

The memory of the man in the white lab coat who threw the fire extinguisher appeared in his mind's eye.

Frank nodded. "I can identify Trey Howard."

"Come with me."

Frank followed the patrolman to the suspect.

The guy turned and glared up at Frank. Brown hair. Dark eyes.

Frank shook his head. "That's not Howard."

"Then who is he?" the cop asked.

"I guess he's who he said he was."

Frustrated by the wild-goose chase, Frank walked back to his car and stared into the distance.

Where was Trey?

SIXTEEN

Duke whined at the door.

"Didn't Frank take you for a walk earlier this morning? He'll be home soon, but I know you want to go out now."

The dog barked.

"You need another romp, right?" She laughed at Duke's attempt to win her heart, which he'd already accomplished.

She unlocked and opened the door. Duke lunged onto the porch and bounded down the steps. He picked up a stick and returned to the open doorway where she stood.

Feeling her mood lighten, she took it from his mouth and threw it into the woods. He scurried off to retrieve the impromptu toy.

Colleen closed her eyes, inhaling the fresh air. The warm breeze brought thoughts of summer vacation when she and Briana were young. Life seemed full of promise then. Now Briana was gone and Colleen was stranded in Freemont.

As a youth, her younger sister had often complained that life wasn't fair. Colleen had known that as soon as Briana had been born. Even at a young age, she'd struggled to accept her curly red hair and had been awed by her sister's beauty right from the start.

Maybe it wasn't fair, but it was also life. Some were given more, some less.

God loves all his children. Words from her Sunday school class played in her mind.

Duke barked.

"Fetch the stick." She opened her eyes.

He barked again.

"Come, Duke."

He refused to obey and stared at something in the woods. A skunk or raccoon? Neither of which she wanted to confront.

"Come on, boy." She slapped her leg as she'd seen Frank do.

Duke growled at the underbrush and held his ground.

The afternoon turned ominously quiet. Birds stopped chirping. Even the cicadas went silent.

Feeling exposed and vulnerable, Colleen stepped back into the house. A sense of relief washed over her as she closed and locked the door. Duke would let her know when he wanted in.

Foolish of her to be so nervous. Trey had been apprehended, and Frank would return soon. She hadn't told him about her being alone when he phoned. He had enough worries.

Once Trey was behind bars, her anxiety would ease, and she'd see everything in a new light.

Then she'd no longer be stranded in Freemont. She would testify when Trey stood trial, but that wouldn't take more than a day or two. He'd trafficked drugs in Atlanta. The trial might be held there. Either way, she would take the stand and tell the truth so that Trey would be stopped forever.

The house phone rang. Maybe it was Frank with news of Trey's arrest.

Evelyn's voice was tight with concern when she greeted Colleen. "Ron's clammy and doesn't remember everything that happened to him. I'm afraid it's his heart. I called an ambulance. Tell Frank when he gets home. Are you sure you're okay?"

"I'm fine. Take care of Ron."

Duke barked.

Colleen returned the phone to the cradle and opened the door to get Duke. She stopped short. A man stood at the foot of the steps, dressed in a red plaid shirt, with a gun in his hand.

Trey.

Taking a step back, Colleen tried to close the door. Trey raced up the steps. His hand reached for her.

She screamed, anticipating his grasp.

Duke snarled, running toward Trey.

"What the—"

He stopped.

Seeing it unfold as if in slow motion, her heart broke.

Trey raised his gun, aimed at Duke and fired.

The dog yelped. His head flew back, his body twisted in air before he fell to the ground.

"No!"

Trey fired again. The shot went wide and hit the side of the porch. Wood splintered.

She pushed on the door that wouldn't close. His foot was wedged across the threshold. She ground her heel into his toes. He growled and lunged.

The door flew open. The force threw her against the table in the foyer. A lamp overturned and crashed to the floor. She ran for the hallway, skidded around the corner.

Frank's room.

His words played through her mind. *Loaded gun... dresser drawer.*

She slammed his bedroom door and turned the lock. Would it hold?

Heart pounding, she pulled open the top drawer on the closest dresser. Socks and underwear neatly arranged. She threw them aside, searching for the gun she couldn't find.

Frantic, she opened a second drawer. T-shirts and running shorts. No weapon.

Crossing the room, she grabbed the phone off the nightstand and yanked on the top drawer of the second dresser.

An army beret. Boxes of military medals. Searching, her hand connected with cold, hard metal.

Relief swept over her. Her fingers wrapped around the grip.

Trey's footsteps sounded in the hallway. He jiggled the knob, pounded on the door.

"I know you're in there, Colleen."

She backed into the bathroom.

He threw himself against the bedroom door. Once, twice.

The wood buckled.

Colleen screamed. Trey crashed into the room.

She slammed the bathroom door. Mouth dry. Heart in her throat. Her hands shook. She could barely turn the lock.

Hitting 9-1-1, she raised the phone and her voice when the operator answered. "This is Colleen Brennan. I'm at Evelyn Gallagher's house just off Amish Road. An intruder with a gun is after me. Send the police. His name is Trey Howard. I'm armed, and I'll shoot if he comes near me."

"Stay on the line—"

Trey threw his weight. The bathroom door flew open.

He stood in the doorway, hair disheveled, eyes wild with fury.

"I'll kill you. Then I'll go to the hospital and finish off Vivian. You can't get away from me. I have too much power. The cops will never believe you. They didn't believe the others."

Like Briana.

He lunged for her.

No time to think. She squeezed the trigger.

Bam!

A deafening explosion. The gun kicked. She flinched. Her ears roared.

Blood darkened Trey's shirt, but he kept coming.

Bam! A second round.

More blood. He grabbed his thigh.

"Why you—" Foul words spewed from his mouth.

Before she could fire again, he turned and hobbled from the bedroom and into the hallway.

Trembling, she stood in the bathroom, unable to breathe, unable to hear anything except for the ringing in her ears.

She slid to the floor, the gun still raised and aimed in case Trey returned. At her feet, she saw spatters of his blood.

SEVENTEEN

Frank saw the police cars as he pulled off the main road and headed back to Evelyn's house. Heart in his throat, he floored the accelerator and screeched into the driveway, where a group of police officers stood. A body lay at their feet.

Colleen? He jumped from the car, pushed through the uniforms and almost cried out when he saw Trey.

"Where is she?"

"Your sister's at the hospital."

His worst fear. "What's her condition?"

"She's fine. Ron Malone may have suffered a heart attack."

"Was he shot?"

"Negative."

"What about Colleen Brennan?"

"She's inside."

Dead or alive? Frank was afraid to ask.

He pushed past two officers in the kitchen, wild to find her.

"Where is she?"

One of the men pointed to the hallway.

Frank tore around the corner. The door to his bedroom lay in pieces. His dresser drawers hung open. Stepping over the clothing scattered on the floor, he saw her.

She was alive.

He ran to where she sat on the bed, her eyes dull, her face pale.

"He hurt you?"

She shook her head and pointed to the bathroom, where two patrolmen were photographing the broken door and blood-covered tiles where his gun lay.

"You shot Trey?"

"He came after me. I called 911. I told them I'd shoot."

"Having the gun saved her life," one of the cops said from the bathroom. "She wounded him in his right arm and left thigh. He stumbled outside just as we pulled into the driveway."

"We warned him to drop his gun," a second officer volunteered. "Instead he opened fire."

The police had taken Trey down, but only after Colleen had tried to protect herself.

"I remembered your gun, Frank."

"Oh, honey, you did the right thing." He pulled her into his arms, feeling the rapid beat of her heart.

Frank hadn't been here to protect her. He should have waited until the cops determined if the guy on the highway was Trey. His impetuousness had almost cost Colleen her life.

He pulled her closer and whispered words of comfort, all the while chastising himself for failing her once again.

Colleen didn't need him. She and the police had taken Trey down. She'd return to Atlanta and her life. What would Frank do?

He inhaled the sweet smell of her hair and pulled her even closer, knowing he had already lost Colleen before he'd even told her how he felt. Her life would go on. Frank would put in his papers to get out of the army and make a new life for himself.

He'd survived without Audrey, but he didn't know if he could survive when Colleen walked out of his life.

"He tried to protect me," Colleen told Frank as he knelt next to Duke.

"Good boy." He rubbed Duke's neck. "You're going to be okay."

Colleen wasn't so sure. The bullet had grazed his hip, leaving him dazed and subdued.

One of the officers had wrapped the wound and placed him on a mat in the kitchen. "It's a makeshift fix, but it'll stop the bleeding until you can get him to the vet."

Footsteps sounded in the hallway. Evelyn rushed into the room. "The police told me."

Her eyes were wide, her face drawn. She reached for Colleen and pulled her close. "Are you okay?"

The embrace, so nurturing, so comforting, brought tears to her eyes. She struggled to blink them back, needing to be strong.

"Duke was hit," she said, her voice heavy with emotion.

"He's a good watchdog." Evelyn squeezed Colleen's arm and stepped toward Frank. She rubbed her hand over his shoulder. "How is he?"

"Probably frustrated that he couldn't take Trey down."

Frank was transferring his own feelings to the dog. Colleen didn't understand his need to be the hero. Trey was dead. Did it matter who had fired the fatal round?

"You'd better get him to the vet," Evelyn suggested. "The police will be here for some time. I'll fix coffee. Colleen can rest."

"Probably a good idea," the cop standing nearby said. "The wound needs to be cleaned. The vet might put him on an antibiotic. You don't want to mess around with a gunshot wound."

Frank glanced at Colleen. "You'll be okay if I leave?"

No, but Duke needed treatment. She didn't want anything to happen to that faithful dog who had tried to protect her. As much as she wanted to go with Frank, she knew there wouldn't be room with Duke stretched out on the passenger seat. Plus, the police would probably have more questions for her to answer.

"Your sister's right. Take Duke to the vet. The danger's passed. Trey can't hurt me now."

Frank loaded Duke in his pickup and drove to the veterinary clinic on post.

"It looks worse than it is," the doc said once he completed his examination. "I'll keep Duke overnight for observation. He should be able to go home tomorrow with a slight limp that will improve with time."

Frank knew about limps and walkers and reprogramming his mind to guard the weakened portion of his body. When Frank had finally walked without relying on a cane, he thought he was ready to go back to work. Then the raging fever and infection had landed him back in the hospital.

"One overnight seems doable." He scratched the scruff on Duke's neck. "You need to stay with the doc tonight."

He licked Frank's hand and laid his head on his paws as if to show he understood.

"See you in the morning, boy." Frank had full confidence in the vet and was grateful Duke was in good hands.

Frank drove across post and parked in front of the CID Headquarters building.

Colby glanced up when Frank entered his cubicle. He looked tired and irritable.

"I take it your wife isn't home yet."

"Becca's temporary duty was extended a few more days."

"Tough break."

Colby nodded. "I wander around the house not knowing what to do when she's not there."

Frank thought of how empty Evelyn's house would seem today without Duke and, even more so, when Colleen returned to Atlanta. It was time for him to find his own place. A small condo that wouldn't bring Colleen to mind.

"I wanted to talk to Wilson. Someone's in his office. I told Sergeant Otis to let me know when he's available."

"Can I help?"

Frank shrugged. "I need to iron out my options."

"You mean when you should come back to work?"

"More or less."

Colby stared at him for a long moment. "I heard what happened. Are you okay?"

"Because Duke was hurt?"

"That and because Trey came after Colleen. I heard she found one of your guns and wounded him."

"All true. He stumbled out of the house and into the sights of the Freemont cops, only he made a fatal mistake and opened fire."

Frank tossed the memory card on Colby's desk. "This is what she took from Trey's office. I thought we needed to take a look."

"She never mentioned a memory card the night we questioned her."

"Colleen wasn't sure she could trust me."

Colby raised his brow and shrugged. "If that's the way you see it."

"You don't?"

"Let's check the photos on the card. We might learn more about why she withheld information."

"A lot had happened. I'm sure she wasn't thinking clearly."

Colby pursed his lips. He didn't appear to accept Frank's explanation.

Sergeant Otis peered into the cubicle. "Sir, the chief can see you now."

"Thanks, Ray."

"While you're talking to Wilson," Colby said, "I'll go over the memory card."

Frank hurried to the chief's office. Wilson was at his desk and glanced up when Frank knocked.

He entered and saluted. "Sir, we need to talk."

Wilson pointed to a chair. "Colby updated me about Colleen Brennan. Sounds like the Freemont police got our man."

Without Frank's help. "Yes, sir. Trey Howard appears to have trafficked drugs into the US. Vivian Davis acted as his mule."

"We haven't been able to question her. The doctor said her condition has improved, but she's still intubated and unable to talk."

"Has her husband provided evidence?"

"Negative. He was completely in the dark. Tough place to be. Redeployed back to Fort Rickman and eager to move to his next duty station at Fort Hood, then his wife is shot and he learns she's been involved in criminal activity." Wilson sniffed. "That's a hard homecoming."

Frank thought of his own medical evacuation back to

the States and his eagerness to see Audrey. "Life isn't always fair."

"Roger that." The chief leaned back in his chair. "Thanks for all your help on the relief effort. Says a lot about you, Frank, that you rolled up your sleeves even though you were still on convalescent leave."

"That's what I want to discuss, sir."

"What's on your mind?"

"Whether I should continue on active duty."

Too much had happened too fast, and Colleen had a hard time trying to come to terms with Trey's death.

She hadn't wanted that for him. She'd wanted him stopped and put behind bars. Now he wouldn't stand trial, and the truth wouldn't come out about his drug-trafficking operation.

The police would consider the case closed and not pursue the other people involved. The whole operation had to be far-reaching, stretching to Colombia and the resort where Trey had invited her to stay.

The memory of Briana played and replayed in her mind. Trey had introduced her to drugs and enticed her to do his bidding, but other folks had worked with him.

Colleen crossed her arms and looked out the French doors beyond the screen porch. Police cars were still parked in the drive, and the crime scene team was finishing up its work.

Evelyn had called a local carpenter who was replacing the doors Trey had broken.

Thinking back to when he'd crashed into the bathroom made her shiver. It all seemed surreal, almost like a dream.

Then she'd been in Frank's arms, feeling his strength and support, which she'd needed. She hadn't wanted to leave his embrace, but he had to take care of Duke. That sweet, faithful dog had done his best to save her from Trey. If Duke took a turn for the worse, she'd never forgive herself.

Tears burned her eyes. Frank had mumbled something about not being there for her. Then he'd left with Duke.

Evelyn had hovered nearby, no doubt sensing Colleen's unease. Although she appreciated Evie's support, Colleen longed to have Frank standing at her side.

Not wanting to answer any more questions, she had retreated to the guest room, claiming she needed rest.

She couldn't relax. All she could do was think back to what had happened and glance at her watch.

What was taking Frank so long?

EIGHTEEN

Frank left the chief's office still unsure of his future. Wilson had listened to the concerns Frank had about his compromised condition. An extended PT program would build him up physically, but a bigger problem was whether he was still an effective investigator. Although Frank hated to admit his limitations, after everything that had happened with Colleen, he was convinced he'd lost his edge.

The chief wasn't known for empathy, but he'd offered advice. "Give yourself more time. Return to active duty, but not to full-blown investigative work at first." Wilson suggested a desk job that wouldn't be as taxing, either physically or mentally.

The thought of pushing papers left a bad taste in Frank's mouth.

He exited the chief's office still unsure of what he should do. The decision didn't get any easier when he faced Colby again.

The other agent was at his desk and pointed to his computer screen. "I've been going over the photos on the memory card."

"What'd you find?"

"It's more like whom." Colby hesitated. "I found Colleen."

Frank nodded. "With a couple guys who work for Trey. She told me all about it. Trey insisted on taking the snapshot. Her refusal would have raised suspicion."

"Not one photo, Frank. Many photos with known drug dealers."

Colby scrolled through the digital pictures and stopped at one that showed Colleen on a couch flanked by two men, neither of whom looked like salt-of-the-earth types.

"Do you recognize those guys?" Colby asked.

"Negative."

Colby provided names. "Atlanta's Narcotics Enforcement Unit said they're bad dudes."

"You called them?"

"And emailed a copy of the photo."

Frank sighed with exasperation. "I told you, Colleen needed to be careful and not raise Trey's suspicion."

Colby shook his head. "I not only question Colleen's judgment but also the other dealers'. Why would they expose themselves to the camera and allow Trey to take their pictures? It doesn't make sense unless they didn't know they were being photographed. Maybe Trey wanted to have the goods on them in case they turned on him. He keeps the photos on the memory card. If the dealers give him a hard time, he's got a way to blackmail them. He could control Colleen that way, too." Colby sniffed. "Isn't that what you thought Vivian and Colleen might be doing with that phone video?"

"Blackmailing Trey?"

"Exactly."

"Vivian could have been, but Colleen just wanted more evidence to prove Trey's guilt."

"If that were the case, she took the wrong memory card. Trey's not in any of these photos."

"What are you trying to say, Colby?"

"I'm saying be careful. Colleen isn't who you think she is."

Frank clamped down on his jaw. The two men had known each other since their early days in the military, but Colby was walking close to the edge of their friendship.

"I'm heading back to Evelyn's."

"I may have it wrong, Frank. Colleen may be innocent, but—" Colby turned back to the monitor and tapped the screen. "In this photo everyone's having fun. Laughing, eating, drinking. Some of them are smoking what looks like weed. The bowls of white powder on the table could be cocaine."

Frank stared at the screen, unable to make sense of what he saw. "Colleen doesn't do drugs. Her sister died of an overdose."

"Which doesn't mean she's not involved. When Briana died, the Atlanta PD thought Colleen might have been her supplier."

"How'd you find that out?"

"Ulster called again. He talked to Anderson."

"Anderson's got it wrong." Frank mumbled a terse goodbye and headed back to his truck, frustrated with Colby.

He thought of the picture he'd seen of Colleen surrounded by a roomful of known criminals.

She was innocent of any involvement with drugs.

Frank was sure of it. Or would Colleen prove him wrong?

Colleen checked the time and then berated herself for being so concerned about Frank. The investigation was winding down, and Frank's attention was back on his job. Trey was dead, and the CID had the memory chip. She was no longer needed.

Grabbing a tissue from the box near the bed, she wiped her eyes and pulled in a cleansing breath before she opened the door.

Evelyn was in the kitchen, making sandwiches that she offered to the police officers who stood nearby.

"May I help?" Colleen wanted to feel useful.

"I thought you were resting."

She looked down at her hands. "I cleaned up a bit, but I couldn't rest. I kept reliving what happened. It's better if I have something to do."

"There's a pitcher of iced tea in the refrigerator. Fill some glasses and see who wants to take a break. The police have been working nonstop."

Pounding came from the hallway.

"That's Zack Barber. He's a retired carpenter from my church. He was nearby, helping to restore one of the Amish farmhouses. He had some spare doors in the back of his truck that hadn't fit the house he was helping to refurbish. He assured me the repairs wouldn't take long."

Colleen poured the tea and kept glancing down, expecting to see Duke. Not having him close by was unsettling. Remembering the reason troubled her even more.

She grabbed a tray from a cabinet and loaded it with the filled glasses.

"I'll be outside."

The officers thanked her profusely as they reached for the refreshing tea. A few followed her back into the kitchen. Evelyn was talking to Ron on the phone and smiled as they helped themselves to the sandwiches she had prepared.

"We'll be finished shortly, ma'am," one of them told

Colleen, his voice low so he wouldn't interfere with Evelyn's phone call.

Colleen had struggled with law enforcement in Atlanta, but these men had come to her rescue when the 911 operator had notified them about the break-in. Their rapid response had stopped Trey and potentially saved her life.

Yesterday, Officer Stoddard, the blond marathon runner, had been considerate when he questioned her. His voice had been filled with compassion, and he made note of everything she told him without raising his brow or shaking his head in disapproval.

Frank had been right. Not all cops were on the take.

As soon as he returned, she'd tell him she'd been wrong. She'd also thank him for inviting her to stay at his sister's house and for helping her track down the memory card. He had protected her at the hospital and again the night Trey had broken into the screen porch as well as at the junkyard.

All Frank focused on was his bad timing, but he'd left Duke to guard the house and had counted on Ron and the loaded gun to ensure her safety. His foresight had allowed her to survive.

She steeled her spine. She could take care of herself. She'd done so in the past and she could again, but when Frank walked into the kitchen, she realized her mistake. She didn't want to go back to Atlanta and be alone again. She wanted what Evelyn and Ron had.

Colleen wanted to smile and laugh and flirt whenever she saw Frank. She wanted to let her eyes twinkle with merriment and joy, which was the same look she'd seen in Evelyn's eyes when Ron was nearby.

Stepping closer to Frank, she asked, "Is Duke okay?"

"The vet said he'll be fine, but he needs to stay overnight for observation."

"I know it was hard for you to leave him." She pointed to the sandwiches. "Evelyn prepared food for the workers. I could pour you a glass of iced tea."

He shook his head. "Don't trouble yourself."

The sharpness in his tone cut her to the core. Why was Frank acting so aloof?

The carpenter lumbered into the kitchen and nodded to Frank. "Tell Evelyn I finished working on those doors. I'll come back in a few days in case she has any other repairs."

When Evelyn got off the phone, she had a lightness to her step, which was a good sign.

After greeting Frank, she shared the news. "The doctor thinks Ron's problem was a lack of potassium. He's been working out recently and probably overdid it being in the sun so long with the relief effort. The doctor ordered more tests for tomorrow, but he's optimistic and so is Ron."

The good news lifted Colleen's spirits. "Are you going back to the hospital?"

"Ron assured me he'll be fine. I'll visit him in the morning."

She stepped closer to her brother. "He wanted to apologize for not coming over while you were gone. I told him he was silly to even give it a thought."

Frank steeled his jaw. "I'm glad Ron's doing better. He doesn't need to worry. Colleen was able to handle the situation."

She stared at him, unable to determine what he meant or what was bothering him.

"I need to talk to the police before they leave." Frank left the kitchen.

Evelyn patted Colleen's hand. "He's struggling because he wasn't here to rescue you."

She shook her head. "There's more to it. It's not about Frank. It's about me."

"Give him a little time. He's still trying to find himself."

Colleen was running out of time. She needed to leave Freemont. Evidently she needed to leave Frank, as well.

NINETEEN

Frank had gotten a full summary of the crime scene investigation from Stoddard before he and the other officers left the area. They had bagged Frank's weapon and had taken blood specimens from the bathroom floor. They'd lifted prints that were probably Trey's and had photographed the entire house.

Once satisfied they'd gotten everything they needed, the police caravan pulled out of the driveway, and Frank headed back inside. Colleen was still in the kitchen, rinsing dishes and placing them in the dishwasher.

"Evelyn's in her room. She looked tired. I told her to get some rest."

"You should, as well."

"As soon as I finish here." She placed a glass in the upper rack. "I…I'm sorry about Duke."

"He'll be fine, I told you."

"Still. I know how close you are."

Frank nodded. "He's a good dog, and he's been a faithful companion. I can trust him."

From the expression on her face, Frank knew his words had hit hard. He wasn't talking about Duke, and she knew it.

More than anything, Frank wanted to believe Colleen. Colby was convinced of her involvement with the drug operation. The pictures proved it. At least that's what Colby thought.

Frank wanted to defend her, which he had tried to do at CID Headquarters. Unfortunately, Colby had already made up his mind. Frank needed information that would prove her innocence without a shadow of a doubt. Information he could shove in Colby's face and take to Special Agent in Charge Wilson.

"Are we back to trust issues again?" she asked.

"Colby found photos of you with a number of known drug dealers." Frank wouldn't mince words. He wanted everything out in the open.

She bristled, immediately on guard. "Haven't we been over this before? I told you about the photo and why I agreed to have my picture taken."

"There were more photos, Colleen. Lots of them showing you fraternizing with drug dealers."

"I wasn't fraternizing."

"What were you doing?"

"Gathering evidence. Just as you do with your investigations."

"I'm trained. You're not. Why didn't you let law enforcement handle it?"

"Because I don't trust cops."

He let out a lungful of hot air. "What about the joints everyone was smoking? The cocaine on the table?"

She shook her head. "I don't know what you're talking about."

"I'm surprised the dealers would let Trey take their photo."

"They might not have known."

"What?"

"One night, I saw him hide a camera behind books

on a shelf by his fireplace and program the shots to snap at a certain time."

"You knew about the secret photos?"

Coleen was digging a bigger hole. One Frank didn't want her to step into because the water in the hole wasn't clear. It had turned a murky brown.

"He didn't see me spying on him. I feigned a headache and went home early that night. I thought that was the only time he'd taken photos on the sly. Evidently I was wrong."

"Did he plan to blackmail the others?"

"I'm not sure. He didn't like people questioning his authority."

"Did he suspect you?"

"Not until I took the memory card."

"Vivian admitted to working for Trey."

Colleen nodded.

"Was she blackmailing him? Is that why you arranged to meet at the roadside park?"

He waited for her to prove him wrong, but she just stared at him. Her cheeks were flushed and her eyes filled with sorrow because she couldn't deny what she knew to be the truth.

Had Colby been right all along?

Frank wanted to hit his hand into his other palm and feel pain for what he'd done to Colleen. He had wanted to prove her innocence. Instead her reticence was telling. His gut twisted. How had he been so wrong?

Colleen turned and hurried down the hall to the guest bedroom. The door slammed, slamming the door to his heart, as well.

Frank was back to when he'd first stumbled upon Colleen in the barn.

He didn't know what to believe.

* * *

Tears burned Colleen's eyes. She couldn't stand there and listen to his accusations any longer. Nothing had changed. Frank didn't see things clearly anymore. Maybe he'd suffered some traumatic brain injury when he'd been caught in the rubble. He couldn't get past thinking she was guilty.

What a fool she'd been to trust him with the memory card and with her heart.

She wouldn't make that mistake again.

Throwing herself on the bed, she cried for all she'd lost. Her sister and now Frank's trust that she'd never had. Tomorrow she'd leave Freemont and head back to Atlanta.

She didn't want to see Frank again. The pain of his betrayal was too deep and too raw. Just as planned, she'd catch a flight to California and never return to Georgia again.

Frank picked up one of the sandwiches on the counter. His stomach was empty, and he needed food, but when he took a bite, it lodged in his throat. How could he have been so mistaken about Colleen?

He checked the doors to ensure they were secure out of habit. Trey would never hurt her again.

Turning off the overhead light, Frank headed to his room, but the thought of what had happened there kept playing in his head.

If he hadn't left a loaded gun—just in case—the night would have had a completely different ending.

At least Colleen hadn't been hurt.

He sat on the edge of his bed and dropped his head in his hands. If Duke were here, the trusty dog would have licked Frank's hand and offered support. His nearness and the understanding in his brown eyes would have brought comfort.

But Duke wasn't here, and Frank had nowhere to turn.

Come back to me.

Words from scripture he'd heard after the storm repeated again in his mind.

He rubbed his forehead. The reconstruction was going well, and the Amish were getting their lives back together while his was falling apart. They were a faithful people who put their hope in God.

He'd stopped relying on the Lord years ago. In those days, the old Frank could take care of himself. He made good decisions and was quickly earning a name for himself in investigation channels. Then he'd made a fateful mistake that nearly cost him his life.

Lord, forgive me for being too haughty, too proud to realize I needed you. The injury and illness opened my eyes to what's important in life, and it isn't good looks or brains and brawn. It's you, Lord. I need you.

His heavy heart weighed him down. He needed Colleen, but not if she was mixed up with drug dealers and trafficking.

Help me see clearly, Lord.

All through the night, Frank sat on his bed and prayed for strength. He'd give himself more time to heal, but he needed clear vision about Colleen.

Was she holding on to things in the past with her sister? Frank realized he was doing the same thing. Audrey was then. Colleen was now.

Opening the drawer on his nightstand, he pulled out a photograph and looked down at the woman with blond hair and blue eyes he had once thought he loved.

He'd been wrong.

True love wasn't about good looks and good times,

and it wasn't easy. It could hurt and get twisted and tied up with other events and other people.

Love was painful. It was now.

He dropped Audrey's photo on his dresser and left the house before Colleen got up. He wanted Duke back at his side, and he wanted to stop by CID Headquarters and review the photos again.

He wouldn't lose Colleen without a fight. Colby had his opinion, but Frank didn't buy it. He believed in Colleen, even if she didn't think he did.

TWENTY

Colleen woke with a pounding headache probably brought on by all the tears she'd shed. After getting dressed, she tidied the room and packed her carry-on bag.

She met Evelyn in the kitchen. "I'm heading to the hospital early. Ron thinks he might be released by noon. I want to talk to the doctors when they make their rounds."

Colleen poured a mug of coffee. "Thanks for all you've done for me. I can't tell you how much I appreciate your kindness."

Evelyn tilted her head. "If I didn't know better, I'd think you were saying goodbye."

"I need to get back to Atlanta. I'd taken a leave of absence from my job. I have to tell them to put me back on the schedule."

"I'm sure Frank will drive you to Atlanta." She smiled. "Something tells me he'll be making quite a few trips into the city in the days ahead."

For all her thoughtfulness, Evelyn didn't realize what had happened last night. Colleen wouldn't tell her.

"I doubt he'll have any spare time once he returns to work. You mentioned a bus station in Freemont."

"The number's in the phone book." She pointed. "First drawer next to the fridge, but I'm sure Frank will find a way to take you himself. You're welcome to stay as long as you like, Colleen. You know Frank and I both enjoy having you here with us."

Evelyn's sincerity touched Colleen. Tears welled up in her eyes. To hide her emotions that seemed so raw this morning, she peered from the window and looked down into the valley.

"The Amish have rebuilt so much, so quickly."

"I'm glad to see it. They help one another and come together as a community."

"The whole town did. It's been encouraging to see."

"I guess you weren't raised in a small town."

Colleen shook her head. "We lived in Savannah and moved to Atlanta soon after my sister was born."

"Small towns take care of their own. From what Frank says, the military is the same way. Maybe even more so since they're often far from family and home."

Family. The word brought another lump to Colleen's throat.

"You've made me feel part of your family, Evelyn. Thank you."

"Why wouldn't we?" She wrapped her arms around Colleen and gave her a hug. "All this talk has me upset, thinking about you leaving."

She pulled back and laughed as she reached for her purse. "I'll expect to see you this evening. I'll bake chicken and have some fresh vegetables. Ron might join us if he feels up to it."

Colleen stood at the door and waved when Evelyn backed out of the drive. Once the car disappeared from sight, Colleen returned to the kitchen and pulled the phone book from the drawer. After finding the number for the bus station, she called and got an automated recording that listed the arrivals and departures. A bus left for Atlanta at ten this morning.

Unsure how long it would take to get to the station, Colleen called for a cab. Returning to her room, she grabbed her carry-on and placed it by the door so she'd be ready when the ride arrived.

Turning, she glanced over the house. So much had happened here. She needed to accept the good along with the bad.

She wanted to retrace the steps she'd taken yesterday so broken doors and blood spatters wouldn't be her last memories of the home. Entering Frank's room, she inhaled the lingering scent of his aftershave and had to close her eyes to keep the tears at bay when she thought of being in his arms.

Peering into the bathroom, she appreciated Zack's workmanship and all that had been done to remove any trace of the tragedy that had unfolded here.

Now Colleen could move on and remember the room as it should be remembered. Leaving the bathroom, she noticed a photo on the dresser.

The picture was of a beautiful blonde with big eyes and an engaging smile that was sure to melt the hardest heart. Curious, Colleen turned the photo over.

To my wonderful Frank. I'll always love you, Audrey.

Colleen dropped the photo and hurried from the room. Frank still loved Audrey. Colleen had been so wrong about everything. He had never wanted anything from her except information.

She hoped he and Audrey could get together again. That would make Frank happy, which is what Colleen wanted for him.

A knock sounded at the front door.

She glanced at her watch. The cab was twenty minutes early. At least she'd get to the bus station ahead of schedule.

She hurried to the foyer and opened the door.

A man. T-shirt. Baseball cap. Not the cabbie.

"Excuse me, ma'am. I'm Steve Nelson."

Frank had mentioned his name. "You're with the construction company here to help with the relief effort."

"That's right." He smiled. "I'm having problems with my cell phone and need to call the mayor's office downtown. We're scheduled to do some demolition today. I was driving by your house when I realized my problem and thought you might be able to help."

"Of course, come in. But it's not my house. I'm just visiting."

He wiped his feet on the doormat and pointed to her carry-on bag as he followed her to the kitchen. "Looks like you're going someplace."

She nodded. "The bus station."

"I'm headed downtown. Let me give you a lift."

"I've already called a cab."

"Easy enough to cancel."

He motioned her to the phone.

She waved him off. "No, you go ahead. Call the mayor."

Grabbing her cell, she checked the coverage. "I'm not having any trouble with my cell reception." Which didn't make sense.

"Really?" He stepped closer. Too close.

Colleen tried to move aside.

He grabbed her arm. "Where's the memory card? Trey said you have it."

"Let me go." She struggled to free herself.

"Trey said you sent a picture to the cops, only it wasn't his operation. It was mine. I need to destroy the memory card."

"You'll never find it."

His grip tightened on her arm. She clawed at his cheek and screamed for help.

The guy pulled a gun. She tried to back away.

"Tell me or you'll die."

"You'll go to jail." Colleen had never seen the photos on the memory card, but she needed something to hold over his head. "Trey took pictures of you that prove your guilt."

Rage twisted his face. "I don't want to hear anything about Trey."

"He outsmarted you," she pressed.

"Shut up." He raised the gun and slammed it against her head.

She gasped with pain.

Darkness settled over her.

Colleen's last thought was of Frank.

TWENTY-ONE

"He had a good night," the vet said when Frank arrived at the clinic.

Duke licked his hand. "I missed you, boy. How's the leg?"

"The wound's healing." The vet handed Frank ointment. "Change the dressing daily and apply more ointment. If it starts to bleed or looks infected, bring him back. Otherwise Duke should be feeling like his old self in seven to ten days."

Frank still didn't feel like his old self, but he appreciated the vet's help, and having Duke by his side made the overcast day seem less gray.

Opening the passenger door, he smiled as the dog hopped into the truck seemingly without effort. "You're going to be chasing squirrels again before long. I'll have to hold you back."

Duke barked. Frank laughed and rounded the car.

"If you don't mind, I want to stop at CID Headquarters and look at some pictures."

The drive across post took fewer than ten minutes. Colby's car was in the parking lot.

"I need to see those photos," Frank said as he entered Colby's cubicle.

"Hey there, Duke." Colby scratched the dog's scruff.

Then he stood and motioned Frank to take his place at the computer.

"Have at it. I'm getting a refill of coffee. Can I get a cup for you?"

"Sounds good. Black."

Frank started scrolling through the photos and stopped when he saw the one Colleen had sent to the police. He enhanced the picture until he could read the name tag on the camera case sitting next to the shrink-wrapped bricks. *Howard.*

Colby came back, carrying two cups. He handed one to Frank.

"Colleen was right about the camera case." He pointed to the monitor. "Looks like it may have belonged to Trey."

"Lots of people are named Howard."

Colby's outlook hadn't improved.

"Has anyone questioned Vivian?" Frank took a slug of the coffee.

"Not yet. The doctor wants to wait another day or two before he weans her off the ventilator."

"And her husband?"

"Faithfully sitting at her bedside."

Frank continued to scroll through the photos, searching for anything that would incriminate the dealers and shed more light on Colleen's innocence.

Colby leaned over his shoulder and sipped his coffee. The process was slow and monotonous.

Many of the shots showed the Colombian resort after its completion. Trey had taken pictures for the travel brochures and advertisements that drew tourists from all over the world. The property was top of the line.

An army wife like Vivian with a deployed husband could easily be swayed by Trey's talk of a modeling career, especially when he included an all-expenses-paid vacation to such a plush resort.

A number of photos showed parties in full swing. Groups of people mixed and mingled, many sipping cocktails. The men were a diverse group. Some wore sport coats; others were in polo shirts and slacks. Attractive women mingled with them, serving drinks and hanging on their arms. Colleen stood to the side, looking very much alone.

Frank's heart went out to her. She hadn't been part of the drug operation. Colleen was an outsider trying to fit in—and failing, in Frank's opinion. It was a wonder Trey hadn't seen through her charade. Determined to bring down the man who had hooked her sister on drugs, Colleen had put herself in danger. Just as she'd told Frank from the beginning, she needed evidence and she found it by infiltrating a large and corrupt drug-trafficking operation.

Frank had to apologize to her for the way he'd acted. She deserved a medal instead of chastisement.

Colby looked at his watch and patted Frank's shoulder. "You keep searching. I've got to be at Post Headquarters in fifteen minutes for a meeting with the chief of staff about the reconstruction. The Freemont mayor will be there to talk about their efforts. The last project is the warehouse demolition by the river."

Frank waved his hand in farewell and glanced down at Duke once Colby had left the room. "Time for us to get going, boy. I need to talk to Colleen and apologize for my actions."

Even with Trey dead, Colleen still needed to be careful, especially if the photos ever got out. Just as she had said, the pictures had served as protection for Trey in case anyone tried to do him harm, but Colleen was front and center. Not a safe place to be.

Frank needed to warn her.

Duke lay his head on Frank's knee, blocking the chair. "What is it, boy? Not ready to leave yet? You like being back at work?"

He chuckled and reached for the mouse. "A few more minutes here won't hurt."

The next section of photos showed the beginning construction effort for the resort. A large sign announced the groundbreaking for La Porta Verde.

Three men stood in front of the sign. A short man with dark skin appeared to be the local contact. Another man, dressed in a flowery Hawaiian shirt, held a stack of papers and must have been part of the initial building project.

A third man shook the Colombian's hand. He was standing to the side, his face in profile. In the distance, a backhoe was poised, ready to break ground.

Frank zoomed in. His gut tightened.

The man in profile was Steve Nelson, the head of the company helping with Freemont's reconstruction.

Frank grabbed his cell and called Evelyn's house.

His sister answered.

"I thought you'd be at the hospital."

"I just got home. Ron's tests came back. The doctor said it was an electrolyte imbalance and released him. I dropped him off at his place and came home to check on Colleen."

"Let me speak to her."

"That's the strange thing, Frank."

He jammed the phone closer to his ear.

"A cab was waiting out front when I pulled up. He said someone needed a ride to the bus station in town."

Colleen was leaving?

"I have to talk to her."

"She's not here."

Frank pushed back from the desk, raced from the cubicle and out the rear door that led to the parking lot. Duke ran beside him.

"I'm on my way to the bus station. If Colleen calls, convince her not to leave town, and tell her she's still in danger."

"You're scaring me, Frank. What's going on?"

"I'll tell you once I find Colleen. What time does the bus leave for Atlanta?"

"Give me a minute to check."

Frank didn't have a minute. He was at his truck. Duke hopped in through the driver's side.

"The bus departs in twenty minutes, but there's something else you need to know."

Climbing behind the wheel, Frank started the ignition. "What is it, Evelyn?"

"Colleen left her carry-on bag by the front door. Her things are strewn all over the floor."

Pain!

Colleen thrashed, trying to escape the burning fire that seared through her head. She moaned, then blinked her eyes open and stared into the damp dimness.

A small room. Table.

She struggled to sit up, realizing too late her hands and feet were bound. A wave of nausea washed over her and sent her crashing back to the musty mattress and pile of rags.

The faint light filtering through the open doorway caused another jolt of pain. She shut her eyes and groaned.

"Coming around?"

A deep voice.

Frank?

She blinked again. Not Frank.

The construction boss. What was his name? Steve. Steve Nelson. Bile rose in her throat as she remembered his attack. "Where…where am I?"

"Someplace safe. At least for now. Where's the memory card?"

"Gone…in the storm."

He bent down, his face inches from hers. His sour sweat and stale breath made her want to gag.

"You only have a few minutes to tell me the truth."

"What…what happens then?"

"Poof!" He threw his hands in the air. "An explosion brings down the building. Tell me about the memory card or you'll die in the blast."

"You're worried. Trey took incriminating photos of you, along with the other dealers." At least she presumed he had.

Steve's eyes widened with fury. "I brought Trey into the operation, but he got greedy and started running his own girls. If the cops hadn't killed him, I would have. They saved me the trouble."

"You're despicable. Trey hooked my sister, Briana, on drugs that caused her to overdose. You're responsible, too."

His lips twisted into a maniacal smile. "Briana wanted out. She went to the cops and told them about Trey. Only one of the cops needed money and passed the information on to me."

Colleen gasped. "You killed my sister."

"She forced my hand. I had to kill her. Just like I have to kill you because you know too much."

"The police have the memory card from Trey's camera. They'll find you and everyone else in your operation. You're finished, Steve."

He shook his head. "I can move to Colombia."

"They'll extradite you back to the States, where you'll spend the rest of your life in jail."

He stepped to the table, leaned over a small gym bag and fiddled with the contents. Nodding to himself as if satisfied with what he'd done, he wiped his hands on his pants and then turned back to her.

"You've got ten minutes. Tell me now or tell me never."

"I'll never tell you anything. The cops will find you and bring you to justice."

"Cops?" He raised his brow. "Or your boyfriend, Frank?"

Her heart lodged in her throat. "He doesn't know anything."

"Of course he does. You gave him the digital card. After I leave the building, I'll go back to his sister's house and wait for him there."

"No." She struggled to free herself.

He turned for the door. All she heard were his footfalls on the old oak floor and his laughter.

Lord, save me. Save Frank.

TWENTY-TWO

Frank left Fort Rickman and increased his speed. River Road wove along the water and led to the older section of downtown Freemont, where the bus station was located. Hopefully Evelyn had phoned Colleen to warn her.

He tried again. All he got was her voice mail.

"Call me, Colleen. Don't leave Freemont. You're in danger."

Which she had been all along. Frank hadn't been able to protect her. He hadn't been there when she'd confronted Trey. Now someone else was after her.

"Steve Nelson is part of the operation in Atlanta," he relayed to her voice mail. "Watch out. I'll be at the bus station in less than five minutes. Stay safe."

After disconnecting, he called Freemont police.

"Head to the old part of Freemont around the bus station. Apprehend anyone wearing an American Construction Company T-shirt or driving one of their vehicles."

He threw the phone on the dashboard and gripped the steering wheel. Pushing down on the accelerator, he willed his truck to go faster. The stretch of road had never seemed so long and so winding.

Frank had been wrong about Colleen. How could he ever prove himself to her?

Lord, forgive me. Lead me to Colleen.

The outskirts of Freemont appeared in the distance.

Although traffic was light, Frank didn't want to stop at intersections in the downtown area. Instead, he remained on River Road. A side street, farther north, would lead to the bus station.

He passed the first of a row of warehouses on his left. The tornado had damaged a portion of the old brick facades on the formidable structures with historic charm.

In days past, boats would unload their wares, and the goods would be stored in the warehouses until wagons transported them to local markets. He didn't have time to bemoan the destruction of a treasure from the past. He needed to find Colleen.

Passing the second building, something caught his eye. He glanced left.

A utility truck sat parked next to a side door.

He stared for half a heartbeat at the company name painted on the van's side panel.

American Construction.

Frank turned the wheel and screeched into the narrow alleyway. He braked to a stop and hit the pavement running.

The big burly guy sat at the wheel. Frank threw open the door. He grabbed Steve's arm and yanked him to the pavement.

The guy reached for the gun tucked in his waistband.

Frank kicked it out of his hand.

"Where is she?"

"You'll never get to her in time." The big guy lunged. His fist jammed into Frank's side, close to his incision.

Air whooshed from his lungs. He doubled over.

Steve stumbled back and grabbed his own gun.

He took aim. "Your girlfriend dies in five minutes, but you die now."

Duke leaped, and his teeth sank into Steve's arm. He screamed with pain. The gun fell from his hand and slid under the van.

The dog didn't let go. Steve toppled backward. His head crashed against the pavement. Gasping in pain, he backpedaled. "Get…the dog…off me."

Sirens sounded nearby.

"Duke, guard." The dog bared his teeth and hovered over Steve. Once big and strong, the construction worker looked like a blubbering baby as he covered his face with his hands and cried.

Frank ran into the warehouse. Shadows played over the expansive area inside. Cobwebs tangled around central support beams and wove their way to the ceiling rafters.

"Colleen!" Her name echoed across the scarred oak floors and bounced off windows fogged with decades of dirt.

Where was she?

Please, God.

He checked his watch. How much time did he have?

Five minutes max.

"Colleen?"

He raced forward. An enclosed office sat in the middle of the giant empty space.

He shoved the door open. A library table, overturned chairs. Two bookcases.

A sound.

Another door.

He turned the knob. The door creaked as it opened. An antique safe stood against the far wall. The room was so dark and so confined that he almost missed the pile of bedding in the corner.

A rustle of movement. Another moan.

He pulled back the blanket and gasped in relief.

Colleen.

Blood matted her beautiful hair and stained the mattress on which she lay. She'd suffered another blow in the same spot. Three strikes.

"I'm here, honey. I'll get you free."

"Explosives…detonate…"

"I know. We don't have much time." Using his pocketknife, he cut through the plastic ties that secured her hands and feet.

He wrapped his arm around her shoulders and helped her to her feet. She faltered.

Half supporting her, half carrying her, he ushered her through the office.

"We have to hurry," he warned.

Sirens sounded outside. Pulsating lights flashed through the filthy windows.

The side door opened. A cop started inside.

"Stay back," Frank shouted. "It's ready to blow."

His side screamed with pain, but he had to save Colleen. She staggered beside him.

Glancing at his watch, his heart lurched. No more time.

"Run." He pushed her toward the open door. She had to get to safety.

The cop grabbed her hand and tugged her through the doorway.

"Take cover," Frank screamed.

He followed her to the threshold of the door. The police had backed off. The cop was ushering Colleen away from the building. She turned, searching for Frank.

Her scream was lost in the blast.

Duke ran toward him.

Frank put up his hand to stop his faithful dog just as an avalanche of bricks started to fall.

Afghanistan. The IED.

Duke wouldn't be able to rescue him this time.

But Frank had saved Colleen.

She was alive.

Nothing else mattered.

"Frank," Colleen screamed.

She fought her way free from the cop who had pulled her from the building. He'd held her back and kept her from Frank.

Duke bounded onto the fallen bricks, the dust thick.

He barked, then sniffed the pile of debris that covered the doorway where Frank had stood seconds earlier.

Now he lay buried beneath the rubble.

She raced forward and clawed at the bricks. Duke dug with his paws, neither of them making progress.

Frank had to be alive. She wouldn't give up hope.

Please God, save him.

Policemen swarmed around them. They shoved aside pieces of brick and piles of dirt that came down with the building.

"Frank, hold on. We'll get you out."

Only she didn't know if he could hear her.

Duke barked. If anything, Frank would hear his trusty dog.

A large beam stretched across the fallen rubble, forming a protective pocket.

If only—

Colleen peered into the opening and glimpsed a hand.

She reached to touch him. Cold. Lifeless.

"Don't leave me, Frank."

His fingers moved.

"He's alive," she shouted. "Hurry."

In a matter of seconds, the cops removed the remaining bricks covering the opening.

Frank's face. Swollen, battered, scraped and bleeding. His eyes shut.

"Watch his neck."

A backboard. They hoisted him carefully onto the wooden brace.

The cops hustled him toward the ambulance.

An EMT approached Colleen and pointed to her forehead. "Ma'am, you need to be examined."

He helped her into the ambulance where two EMTS worked on Frank. She sat opposite them and took his hand. She wouldn't let go.

Duke climbed in beside her.

The doors closed, and the ambulance took off, siren screaming.

Colleen couldn't stop watching the rise and fall of Frank's chest. He was breathing. He was alive, but just barely.

TWENTY-THREE

Although his prognosis wasn't good, Colleen was so grateful Frank was still alive. His condition was critical when he was raced into the Fort Rickman Hospital emergency room yesterday.

An entire medical team had worked on him in the trauma room until a bed opened in the ICU. Since then, he'd been hooked to wires that monitored his pulse, oxygen level, heart rate and blood pressure.

The occasional beep and the thrust and pull of the medical machinery made Colleen even more anxious about his condition.

She'd sat by his side throughout the night. Evelyn said she would stay, but fatigue had increased her limp and her eyes lacked their usual sparkle. She had been worried about Ron. Now her concern was for her brother.

"Go home, Evelyn. Sleep. You can spell me in the morning," Colleen had told her.

Civilians weren't usually treated at military hospitals, but one of the emergency room docs had checked Colleen over. Another slight concussion. Her third. The doc laughed as he said that she'd struck out. At least he didn't seem overly concerned, especially since she planned to stay the night at Frank's bedside.

The RN on duty had provided blankets and showed

her how the vinyl chair extended into a semiflat position. Colleen had tried to sleep, but with the constant flow of medical caregivers who checked on Frank, she'd dozed off only a few times and then not for long.

The morning-shift nurse had provided a sealed plastic container of toiletries that included a toothbrush and comb. Colleen had given up trying to bring order to her matted hair and had used a rubber band to pull her unruly locks into a makeshift bun that at least got the curly strands out of her face.

Since first light, she'd hovered close to Frank's bedside, watching in case his eyes opened. She'd prayed throughout the night that God, who heard all, would answer her request and restore Frank to health.

"If he does respond," the doctors cautioned, "a full recovery will take time."

She sighed as the weight of that one comment sank in. If he recovered? A full recovery will take time? How long?

It didn't matter. She'd wait forever, if Frank wanted her to stay. That was the problem. She didn't know what he wanted.

She glanced at the floor, wishing Duke were with her. The military doctors hadn't been as welcoming as the EMTs in the ambulance had been. As soon as Ron and Evelyn arrived at the hospital, they'd been instructed to take the dog home.

A knock sounded. The door to Frank's room opened, and a man in uniform entered. He was tall with a full face and gentle smile.

"I'm Major Hughes, one of the chaplains on post."

"Thank you for coming."

He glanced at Frank. "Mind if I say a prayer?"

She rose from the chair. "Of course not. Yours might bring better results than mine."

"You've had a long night. The nurse told me you've been at his bedside."

"Praying." She tried to smile, but tears filled her eyes. She didn't want to cry in front of the chaplain.

He reached for her hand. "God knows our hearts. He responds. Although sometimes he's not as timely as we'd want."

"That's what worries me."

"We need to trust."

She nodded. Her weak suit, especially when it came to Frank. "He's a good man. Compassionate, caring, but he's been through so much."

"I was told a war injury and multiple surgeries followed by a life-threatening infection."

Colleen nodded. How much could someone endure? "He ignored his own condition to help me. I…I made a mistake and wasn't completely forthright."

She turned her head and bit her lip.

The chaplain patted her shoulder. "Our limitations are always easier to see in hindsight. When we're in the middle of a stressful situation, our vision is often cloudy. The Lord is a God of forgiveness. You can trust him." He glanced at Frank. "I have a feeling you can trust Special Agent Gallagher, as well."

Buoyed by the chaplain's words, she folded her hands and bowed her head as he prayed, knowing God was in charge. He was the Divine Physician who would return Frank to health.

That was her hope.

That was her prayer.

* * *

Someone patted Frank's arm. He heard voices and tried to comprehend what they were saying.

"I think he's coming around."

Evelyn?

He sensed someone else bending over his bedside. "Agent Gallagher? Frank? Can you hear me?"

He fought his way from the darkness.

"Open your eyes?"

He tried. They remained shut.

"My name's Molly. I'm the nurse who's taking care of you today. You're in the hospital at Fort Rickman. Do you remember what happened?"

He turned his head.

"Open your eyes, Frank." Evelyn's voice. She patted his hand.

Still so tired, but he wanted to see—

Light. Too bright.

"That was great. Try opening your eyes again."

He blinked. Twice.

"Even better. Keep working. I bet your eyes are blue."

Brown. He licked his lips, but the word wouldn't form.

"Eyes opened wide. That's what I want to see."

Again, he blinked against the light. The nurse smiled down at him.

He turned his head ever so slightly. Evelyn came into view.

"Oh, Frank," she gushed. A tear ran down her cheek. "I've been so worried."

She squeezed his hand. He squeezed back.

"Wh…where—"

Slowly, his gaze swept the room. A knife stabbed his heart. He had expected to see Colleen.

Audrey had left him. Now Colleen.

He didn't want to keep struggling any longer. He was worn-out and unwilling to fight back from the brink of despair again.

He had almost died last time. He wasn't willing to bear the hurt again.

"Keep your eyes open, Frank."

He ignored the nurse and slipped back into the darkness, where he couldn't feel pain. Why should he open his eyes? He didn't want to see anything if he couldn't see Colleen.

"You need to go back to my place and get some sleep," Evelyn suggested.

Colleen shook her head. "The last time I stepped out for coffee, Frank opened his eyes. I want to be here next time."

"If there is a next time," Evelyn said. Her voice contained all the fear Colleen felt.

She shook her head. "Don't say that."

"The doctors warned us. We need to realize what could happen."

"God won't take him from me. I've lost Briana. I can't lose Frank."

Evelyn rubbed her shoulder. "Life isn't always fair."

Colleen nodded. How well she knew that to be true.

She thought of Evelyn's first love and the pain she'd experienced when he revealed the truth about his marriage.

"You've had your share of suffering."

"But now I have Ron."

"Did you tell him about Dan?"

Evelyn nodded. "Just as you mentioned, he was loving and caring. Although like a typical male, Ron wanted to punch Dan. Even if he hadn't been married, what he and I had wasn't true love. It was something that fell far short. Looking back, I know God saved me for Ron."

Colleen squeezed Evelyn's hand. "I wasn't sure about Ron because of seeing him with Trey the night of the tornado, but I was wrong, too. He's got a big heart and a lot of love to shower on you, Evelyn."

She glanced at her brother. "Frank does, too. He just needs to wake up and accept your love."

The phone rang. Evelyn reached for the receiver. "Yes?"

She smiled. "You're downstairs? I'll be right there." She hung up and patted Colleen's hand.

"Ron's in the lobby. I'm going to meet him for coffee in the cafeteria. Can I bring you anything?"

"Bring your brother back, and I'll be happy."

"Ron and I are praying. The whole church community is, as well."

Would it be enough? Colleen wasn't sure.

Colleen heard Frank's voice in her dream. She smiled and squeezed his hand.

"Ouch."

Her eyes popped open. Sitting in the chair at Frank's bedside, she had rested her head on the edge of his mattress and dozed off.

His eyes were still closed. Her dream had been so real. Had she imagined his voice?

Maybe the three strikes were finally catching up to her.

She rubbed her hand over his. His fingers moved.

Her heart skittered in her chest.

"Frank?"

One eye blinked open.

The IV solution was providing fluids, but that didn't keep his lips from being cracked and chapped.

"C…ol…leen?"

Surely he didn't think she was Audrey.

His smile widened. His fingers wrapped through hers. "You…you…didn't leave me."

"Oh, Frank, I'll never leave you."

Tears filled her eyes and spilled down her cheeks.

She moved closer to him. His other eye opened. "Now…I…see you."

"I haven't even combed my hair."

"You…you're beautiful."

"Do you remember what happened?"

He nodded ever so slightly. "I…saved…you."

She smiled. "That's exactly right. You saved my life."

His brow wrinkled. "D…Duke?"

"He's fine. Evelyn claims his sense of smell returned, since he was able to find you in the rubble. I'm sure you heard him barking."

Frank wrinkled his forehead. "I…I heard…your voice. You…gave…me…will to live."

"Oh, Frank, I was so wrong about you and about law enforcement. You were trying to find the truth, and I kept holding back information."

The words gushed out. Colleen couldn't stop them. "Briana's death had taken me to the depths of despair. I'd turned my grief into a need to bring all those involved with drug trafficking to justice."

She shook her head, frustrated at her own actions. "Only I was headstrong and foolish to take on Trey and his operation. You kept trying to protect me, but I wasn't sure of where I stood with you. I'd been so determined to bring Trey down that I almost got myself killed and you killed, as well."

Frank rubbed her hand. "Before…thought I was invincible…didn't need God…didn't need anyone. Dated a girl. She…must have known. Only person…I…I…loved was my…self."

"You're not that man any longer. You're not self-serving or self-centered. You're a wonderful man who has a bright future ahead in law enforcement. You check every detail and make sure hearsay isn't taken as fact. I thought Trey had caused Briana's death, but Steve Nelson was to blame. I went after the wrong man."

"Trey…led you to Steve."

"You're right. Colby stopped by after work last night. He said the photos on the memory card revealed even more drug dealers involved in Steve Nelson's far-reaching operations. The resort is being cleaned out in Colombia, and the DEA is going after traffickers throughout the Southeast. Colby called it a good day for law enforcement."

"Be…cause of you."

"Because you helped me find the memory card."

Frank smiled.

"Colby said Anderson, the cop I contacted in Atlanta, was tied in with Trey. He's been arrested."

"Vi…vian?"

"She confessed to smuggling drugs into the US and provided information about others involved. Colby said the judge will take that into consideration."

"I'm…sorry…I…"

She smiled. "Didn't believe me?"

He nodded.

"You were being that wonderful investigator who I'm beginning to think I love."

His eyes opened a bit wider, and the smile that filled his face made her heart soar with joy.

"I…love…you, Colleen."

Her grip tightened on his hand, and she bent over his bedside. His condition was still fragile, and he had a long recuperation ahead, but Colleen wanted him to know the way she felt. She had waited too long to tell him the truth.

"I love you, Frank."

She gently lowered her lips to his, and for one long moment the earth stood still.

Pulling back ever so slightly, she added, "And I'll never leave you." She smiled. "Cross my heart."

His eyes closed, and he fell back to sleep. Resting her cheek against his hand, she gave thanks to God for bringing this wonderful, strong man into her life.

TWENTY-FOUR

Frank sat on Evelyn's front porch and listened for the sound of tires on the driveway. Seeing Colleen's new red Mustang convertible, he hurried down the steps and opened her door as she pulled to a stop.

Before either of them spoke, he reached for her and pulled her into his arms. Their lips met, and the lingering kiss did more for him than all the physical therapy he'd been having over the past five weeks.

Evelyn stood in the open doorway and waved. Duke bounded around her and barked with glee, causing Colleen to push away from Frank and laugh.

"Are you jealous of Frank?" she asked as the dog danced at her feet. She patted his sleek coat and scratched behind his ears.

"How was your flight?" Evelyn asked from the porch.

"Easy. I'm enjoying working short domestic flights again."

"And we like having you spend time between trips with us."

Frank grabbed her carry-on from the backseat. "The Mustang suits you."

"Oh? Is it the color?"

"You mean because it matches your hair?"

She laughed. "I didn't think you noticed."

"I notice everything about you."

"Be still my heart. I like having a man who's observant."

"And I like your hair loose around your face. It suits you just like the car."

He ran his hand through the curls that fell free around her shoulders. Leaning close, he inhaled the flowery scent of her shampoo, which made him want to kiss her again.

She giggled. "Looks like you're feeling better. Did you talk to Wilson?"

"He's wants me back doing CID investigations as soon as I'm ready."

Colleen narrowed her gaze. "What'd you tell him?"

"Next Monday. I'm ready."

She nodded. "I know you are."

"What smells so good?" Colleen asked as they followed Evelyn into the kitchen.

"I've got a rib roast in the oven, and Isaac selected fresh corn from the Amish Craft Shoppe for us, along with homegrown lettuce and an apple pie for dessert."

"You always spoil me, Evelyn."

"Ron's joining us for dinner."

"How's he feeling?"

"Strong as an ox."

Colleen laughed. "Is he still working out?"

Evelyn nodded. "He has to keep in shape to keep up with me." She winked at Colleen, who laughed again.

Her joy was infectious, and Frank's heart soared. "Let's go for a drive."

She looked confused. "I…I just got here."

"I know, but there's something I want to show you."

She glanced at Evelyn, who smiled knowingly but didn't say anything.

He took her hand and hurried her to his truck. He

held the passenger door for her, and lowered the back for Duke. They were soon heading along the country road they'd traveled weeks before.

They passed Dawson Timmons's house. Frank turned at the next intersection and headed north for a little over three miles.

"This area is so beautiful." Colleen's smile said as much as her comment.

He stopped at the top of a small rise and helped her out. Duke jumped from the rear and immediately chased after a gray squirrel that scurried up a sturdy oak.

Frank pointed to a small pond and the gentle rise where more hardwoods grew.

"I thought a house overlooking the pond might be nice. The trees would provide shade in summer."

Her eyes widened with surprise. "You're buying the land?"

"I went to the bank, but I haven't signed the papers yet."

"Does that mean you're getting out of the army?"

"Not now. I've got ten years on active duty already. I'll stay in for at least ten more before I retire from military service. I thought farming the land, raising a few head of cattle, might be something for the future. I'll live here for the next three years while I complete my assignment at Fort Rickman. When I'm transferred, I'll still need a place to come back to for vacations and to visit Evelyn."

Colleen turned to look at the expanse of land. "It's lovely. A good place to call home."

"How would you feel about living here?"

She took a step back. "I'm not sure what you're saying."

He laughed, realizing his mistake. "Looks like I got ahead of myself."

Digging into his pocket, his fingers touched a small box. He pulled it out. "I'm not overly romantic, and I may not have the right words, but I love you, Colleen. You're my everything, and I never want to spend a day without you. Will you—"

He opened the box. "Will you marry me?"

Colleen's heart stopped for a long moment as Frank removed the solitaire diamond and held it out ready to put on her finger.

"Will you marry me?" he asked again when she failed to respond.

Tears filled her eyes. She brushed them away, knowing her cheeks would blotch and her mascara would run, but she didn't care. All she cared about was Frank.

"Yes," she almost screamed, holding out her hand. He slipped the ring over her finger, then he pulled her into his arms.

"I love you."

"Oh, Frank, I love you, too."

They kissed under the shade of the oak tree. Duke fetched a twig and raced back to where they stood, wrapped in each other's arms. He danced at their feet, trying to get their attention until another squirrel caught his eye. Then he bounded off in pursuit, while Frank pulled Colleen even closer, and she nestled in his arms.

His kisses were as sweet as the wildflowers blooming on the hillside and as warm as the sunshine overhead.

This land, their home, would be the perfect place to seal their love and raise a family.

Colleen glanced at the ring and then raised her lips

again to the wonderful man, the strong and determined man with whom she planned to spend the rest of her life.

God had answered her prayers. Every one of them.

* * * * *

Dear Reader,

I hope you enjoyed *Stranded*, the seventh book in my Military Investigations Series, which features heroes and heroines in the army's Criminal Investigation Division.

Each story stands alone so you can read them in any order, either in print or as an ebook: *The Officer's Secret*, book 1; *The Captain's Mission*, book 2; *The Colonel's Daughter*, book 3; *The General's Secretary*, book 4; *The Soldier's Sister*, book 5; and *The Agent's Secret Past*, book 6.

In this story, Special Agent Frank Gallagher is ready to return to duty after recuperating from a war injury when a tornado drops flight attendant Colleen Brennan into his life. She's running from a drug trafficker and doesn't trust law enforcement. Frank fears he's lost his edge and doesn't know if he can trust his investigational ability or his heart.

I want to hear from you. Email me at debby@debbygiusti.com or write me c/o Love Inspired, 233 Broadway, Suite 1001, New York, NY 10279. Visit my website at www.DebbyGiusti.com and blog with me at www.seekerville.blogspot.com.

Wishing you abundant blessings,

Debby

COMING NEXT MONTH FROM **Love Inspired® Suspense**

Available April 7, 2015

DUTY BOUND GUARDIAN
Capitol K-9 Unit • by Terri Reed

A stolen art relic leads K-9 officer Adam Donovan to Lana Gomez as the prime suspect. Yet when the true thief tries to kill Lana, Adam must safeguard the gorgeous museum curator.

SECRET REFUGE
Wings of Danger • by Dana Mentink

The man who killed Keeley Stevens's sister is now threatening Keeley. Former parole officer Mick Hudson knows it's up to him to keep her out of harm's way and bring the criminal to justice.

TARGETED • by Becky Avella

Despite his recent injury, officer Rick Powell is determined to keep schoolteacher Stephanie O'Brien from becoming a serial killer's next victim.

ROYAL RESCUE • by Tammy Johnson

Ever since her father's murder, princess Thea James has lived in fear. Royal bodyguard Ronin Parrish promises he'll shield her from the attacker, but does he have ulterior motives?

PRESUMED GUILTY • by Dana R. Lynn

Framed for a crime she did not commit, Melanie Swanson must now trust a handsome policeman to protect her from becoming the real criminal's next target.

FATAL FREEZE • by Michelle Karl

Trapped aboard an icebound ferry with a dangerous crime ring, private investigator Lexie Reilly and undercover CIA agent Shaun Lane will need to work together if they want to survive.

SPECIAL EXCERPT FROM

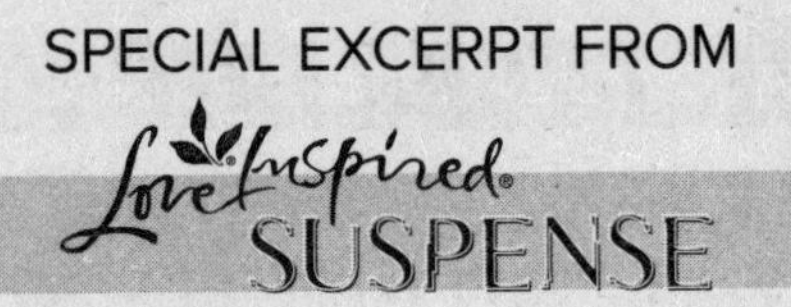

Framed for a crime she didn't commit, museum curator Lana Gomez must prove her innocence under the watchful eyes of Capitol K-9 Unit officer Adam Donovan.

Read on for a sneak preview of the next exciting installment of the ***CAPITOL K-9 UNIT*** *series,* *DUTY BOUND GUARDIAN* *by* Terri Reed.

K-9 officer Adam Donovan's cell buzzed inside the breast pocket of his uniform shirt. He halted, staying out of the rain beneath the overhang covering the entrance to the E. Barrett Prettyman Federal Courthouse.

"Sit," he murmured to his partner, Ace, a four-year-old, dark-coated, sleek Doberman pinscher. The dog obediently sat on his right. Keeping Ace's lead in his left hand, he answered the call. "Adam Donovan."

By habit Adam scanned the crowds of tourists flooding the National Mall, on alert for any criminal activity. Not even nighttime or an April drizzle could keep sightseers in their hotels. To his right the central dome of the US Capitol building gleamed with floodlights, postcard perfect.

"Gavin here" came the deep voice of his boss, Captain Gavin McCord. "You still at the courthouse?"

LISEXP0315

Adam had had a late meeting with the DA regarding a case against a drug dealer who'd been selling in and around the metro DC area. The elite Capitol K-9 Unit had been called in to assist the local police during a two-hour manhunt nine months ago. The K-9 unit was often enlisted in various crimes throughout the Washington, DC, area.

Ace had been the one to find the suspect hiding in a construction Dumpster outside of the National Gallery of Art. The suspect took the DA's deal and gave up the names of his associates rather than stand trial, which had been scheduled to begin later this week.

A victory on this rainy spring evening.

"Yes, sir."

"There's been a break-in at the American Museum and two of the museum employees have been assaulted," Gavin stated.

"Injured or dead?" Adam asked, already moving down the steps toward his vehicle with Ace at his heels.

"Injured. The intruder rendered both employees unconscious, but the security guard came to and pulled the fire alarm, scaring off the intruder. Both have been rushed to the hospital on Varnum Street." Gavin's tone intensified. "But the other victim is who I'm interested in. Lana Gomez."

LISEXP0315

SPECIAL EXCERPT FROM

Can Mary find happiness with a secretive stranger who saves her life?

Read on for a sneak preview of the final book in Patricia Davids's ***BRIDES OF AMISH COUNTRY*** *series,* *AMISH REDEMPTION.*

Hannah edged closer to her. "I don't like storms."

Mary slipped an arm around her daughter. "Don't worry. We'll be at Katie's house before the rain catches us."

It turned out she was wrong. Big raindrops began hitting her windshield. A strong gust of wind shook the buggy and blew dust across the road. The sky grew darker by the minute. She urged Tilly to a faster pace. She should have stayed home.

A red car flew past her with the driver laying on the horn. Tilly shied and nearly dragged the buggy into the fence along the side of the road. Mary managed to right her. "Foolish *Englischers*. We are over as far as we can get."

The rumble of thunder became a steady roar behind them. Tilly broke into a run. Hannah began screaming. Mary glanced back and her heart stopped. A tornado had dropped from the clouds and was bearing down on them. Dust and debris flew out from the wide base.

Dear God, help me save my baby. What do I do?

She saw an intersection up ahead.

Bracing her legs against the dash, she pulled back on the lines, trying to slow Tilly enough to make the corner without overturning. The mare seemed to sense the plan. She slowed and made the turn with the buggy tilting on two wheels. Mary grabbed Hannah and held on to her. Swerving wildly behind the horse, the buggy finally came back onto all four wheels. Before the mare could gather speed again, a man jumped into the road waving his arms. He grabbed Tilly's bridle and pulled her to a stop.

Shouting, he pointed toward an abandoned farmhouse. "There's a cellar on the south side."

Mary jumped out of the buggy and pulled Hannah into her arms. The man was already unhitching Tilly, so Mary ran toward the ramshackle structure. The wind threatened to pull her off her feet. The trees and even the grass were straining toward the approaching tornado. She reached the old cellar door, but couldn't lift it against the force of the wind. She was about to lie on the ground on top of Hannah when the man appeared at her side. Together, they were able to lift the door.

A second later, she was pushed down the steps into darkness.

LIEXP0315